THE WORLD
OF THE
GIANT PANDA

Also by Richard Perry:

AT THE TURN OF THE TIDE
THE WORLD OF THE JAGUAR
THE WORLD OF THE WALRUS
THE UNKNOWN OCEAN
THE POLAR WORLDS

Richard Perry

THE WORLD
OF THE
GIANT PANDA

with illustrations by Wolfgang Weber

TAPLINGER PUBLISHING COMPANY
NEW YORK

599.7
P464w

New Printing 1972

First published in the United States in 1969 by
TAPLINGER PUBLISHING CO., INC.
New York, New York

Copyright © 1969 by Richard Perry
All rights reserved. Printed in the U.S.A.

No part of this book may be reproduced or transmitted in any
form or by any means, electronic or mechanical, including
photocopy, recording, or any information storage and retrieval
system now known or to be invented, without permission in
writing from the publisher, except by a reviewer who wishes
to quote brief passages in connection with a review written for
inclusion in a magazine, newspaper or broadcast.

Library of Congress Catalog Card Number: 75-79851

ISBN 0-8008-8585-6

Ling-Ling at the National Zoo, Washington, D.C.

34111

Acknowledgements

Once again I am much indebted to Maurice Michael for translations of a number of scientific papers; and to the Cornwall County Library for supplying me with numerous books. Also to the Librarian and the map-room staff of the Royal Geographical Society; and to the Zoological Society of London for a transcript of the tape-recording made in Moscow during the affair of Chi-Chi and An-An.

For permission to quote from original sources I have to thank the following publishers and authors: Hutchinson, *Men and Pandas* (1966) by Ramona.& Desmond Morris; *Animals*, 'Zoos in China' (1966) by Caroline Jarvis; *Field*, 'Five Giant Pandas' (1938) by R. Loseby and 'In Quest of the Giant Panda' (1935) by Dean Sage.

The illustrations at the head of each chapter were drawn by Wolfgang Weber for an article in *Zoologischer Garten* magazine, Leipzig, by Dr Gerhard Haas. I am most grateful to artist, author and publisher for permission to reproduce them here.

CONTENTS

I passionately love the beauties of Nature; the marvels of the hand of God transport me with such admiration that in comparison the finest work of man seems only trivial.

Abbé David

Introduction

In this, the fourth of my studies of the great mammals, I ought perhaps to explain that I began my researches solely for my own interest, at a time when I was not actively writing for publication, because I was unable to find any fully comprehensive or coherent accounts of their life-histories in English, nor apparently in any other language; and because I felt very strongly that I should do this while some of these mammals were still to be found in the wild state.

As chance would have it, I had almost completed the MS of the first of these studies, *The World of the Tiger,* for my personal satisfaction when Maurice Michael, who had found me a publisher for *The Watcher and the Red Deer* some ten years earlier, happened to contact me to inquire whether I had any MSS on the stocks after my long silence. I am grateful to him and to Cassell, who felt that other people besides myself might be interested in these life-histories of mammals which, so far as one can judge, are doomed as *wild* animals in this era of the human population explosion and its attendant militant aggression; and I should perhaps add that the scope of my interest is precisely defined in the general title of the series.

Tigers, polar bears and walruses were all in need of a biographer, as is the jaguar; and so were giant pandas when I began my researches into their life-history. In the interim, however, Ramona and Desmond Morris have published their very fully documented *Men and Pandas;* but it was decided that as I was primarily concerned with the giant panda as a wild animal I should continue with my study, which owes much to the Morrises' spadework.

RICHARD PERRY
Dartmoor 1968

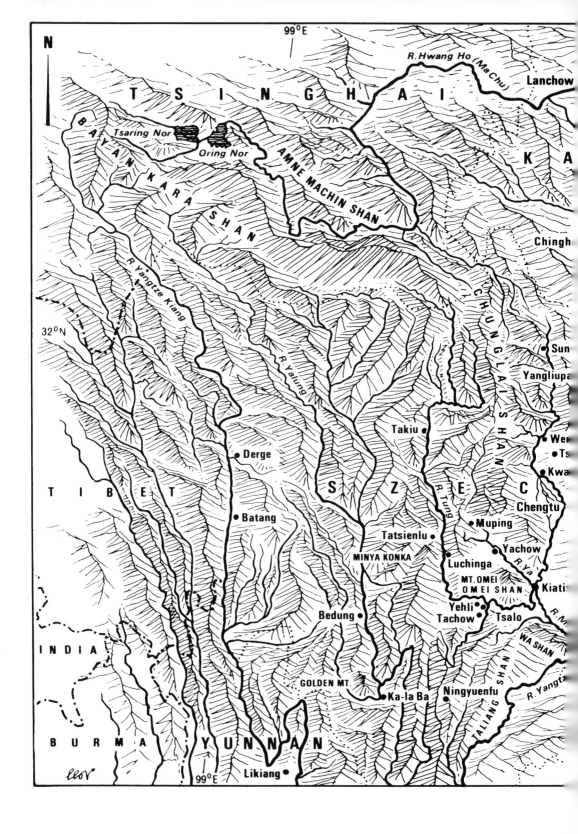

CHAPTER ONE

His World

What is this world of the giant panda?

To the west – parallel range upon range of gigantic mountains, older than the Himalayas, curving south from the Tibetan high-lands to culminate in the razor-backed ridges and deep, narrow ravines of Yunnan. To the north – the steppes and desert of Mongolia. Eastwards – beyond the mountain gorges of the Min river's rushing blue waters and foaming rapids, the great red plain of Szechwan, with its teeming peasant millions, and the swirling Yangtze.

1

Within these geographical boundaries is a natural sanctuary, as rugged and inaccessible to explorers and big-game hunters as almost any in the world: an inconceivably complex escarpment, in which it is the unfathomable depths of the ravines, rather than the towering snow-clad peaks empounding them, that impress the traveller. Only the eagles, soaring and wheeling high above the crags, can look down into the black shadows of these abysses. The transition from the floor of these ravines and valleys to the Tibetan steppes, several thousand feet above, is so abrupt that in a few hours the naturalist finds himself passing from the sub-tropical through the temperate into the alpine zone.

To the Tibetans, this is *Ngam-grog-chi*, which might be translated as 'the Land of the Deep Corrugations'. To the Chinese, *Hsi-fan*, 'the Land of the Western Barbarians'. To the Europeans, some of the most difficult country on Earth where, if one does not follow the regular trails, it may take a month to cover fifty miles.

'The country where I find myself and where I am thinking of staying for almost a year,' wrote the Jesuit missionary Père David on 21 March 1869, from the Lazarist college in Muping, at the headwaters of the Ya river in north-west Szechwan, 'is a frightening region of steep and craggy mountains, heaped up one upon the other – the beginning of the high Tibetan plateau. Peaks of perpetual snow raise themselves not far from here . . . Although we are below 30 or 31, winter has hardly begun to leave us and snow still covers a great part of the country.'

Four days earlier Jean Pierre Armand David – possibly the first Westerner to see a giant panda dead or alive – had made a very difficult excursion to explore the mountain of Hongchatin, which dominated Muping. In his diary he described how:

Leaving the college at seven in the morning, Ovang Thomé [his servant, 'Yellow Tom'] and I go up into a wild valley of the famous mountain. Toward eleven, following the rugged banks of the still half-frozen stream, we reach the foot of a series of splashing, foaming cascades, where the narrow foot-path we have been following to that point suddenly stops. After we have eaten our crust of bread moistened with icy water, we try to climb the steep mountain on either side of this narrow valley, hoping to find a passage over the difficult cascades, but

The approaches to Hsi-fan – a typical landscape in central Szechwan. *(J. Allan Cash)*

in vain. For four whole hours we pull ourselves up from rock to rock as high as we can go by clinging to trees and roots. All that is not vertical is covered with frozen snow. These immense steep walls are capable of frightening the boldest. But after we have reached a certain height it becomes impossible to ascend without slipping and falling on the ice. We are badly scratched and our clothes and equipment are soaked. Our strength is exhausted as never before. Sometimes we are plunged into half-melted snow, or the trees which we clutch break and we roll to another tree or near-by rock.

The inconceivable difficulties of this monkey-like ascent absorb us so much that we pay no attention to the fresh traces of several large animals on the snow. And that too is dangerous, for it is a matter of fierce bears and wild bulls [takin] which, it is said, the mountaineers fear more than leopards and even tigers. We pay no attention to striped squirrels jumping slowly among the beard-lichens hanging from branches of centenarian pines, nor to the noisy nutcrackers which haunt these high forests.

At last the sun, which has shone till three o'clock, disappears in the thick fog, in which we are soon lost. Being utterly exhausted we are forced to descend, so as not to be overtaken by night in these awful solitudes. No sound breaks the silence, except the distant noise of the cascades and the plaintive croaking of the brown carrion crow. I also distinguish the distant lowing of a wild ox.

We descend the immense wall of over three thousand feet the same way we have climbed it, namely from tree to tree and rock to rock. Often the sides of the mountain are vertical.

But if the climate of Hsi-fan can be harsh, it is a very beautiful sanctuary, comparable in the majesty of its scenery and the wealth of its wildlife to the paradise of the Tien Shan. For the giant panda's haunts are also those of the little red panda and of the extraordinary golden or snow monkey, with its silky mane of golden hair twelve or eighteen inches in length and its snub nose resembling a bright blue butterfly sitting with open wings in the middle of its face; of bears and lynxes and various small tiger-cats

4

and three species of leopard – spotted, snow and clouded – and maybe even an occasional wandering tiger; of the prey of these carnivores – the sambar and white-lipped deer, tufted deer, muntjac and musk deer, and those peculiar creatures that are neither antelopes nor goats, the takin, the goral and the serow; and of the world's most resplendent varieties of gorgeous pheasants and tropagons.

The boundaries of Hsi-fan, it will be noted, range only a degree or two above and below 30° north latitude. Elsewhere in the world this is a sub-tropical zone, including such hot spots as Pakistan, Iraq, North Africa, Florida and California. And Hsi-fan itself must have enjoyed a sub-tropical climate before tectonic forces began throwing up twenty-thousand-foot mountains. No doubt this climacteric proved too severe for many of Hsi-fan's original inhabitants, forcing some species to emigrate to more congenial regions and resulting in others' becoming locally extinct; but a few natives, such as the giant panda, were able to adapt themselves to these vastly different climatic conditions and remain in Hsi-fan.

This new Hsi-fan was not completely imprisoned by mountain ranges. High passes through them gave access to the Tibetan Himalayas and steppes in the north and west; and riverine valleys, such as that of the Mekong, opened the way to south-east Asia. By these routes there came into the new Hsi-fan takin and goral and a variety of smaller mammals, to share the high bamboo jungles and coniferous forests with the giant panda.

The precipitous mountainsides that enclose all the valleys in Hsi-fan are zoned with broad bands of almost impenetrable bamboo jungle, extending from 5,000 or 6,000 to 10,000 or 12,000 feet. In the open forests of silver fir the bamboo grows as scrub to a height of six or eight feet, but to twelve or fifteen feet in sparsely timbered belts. Intolerant of overhead shade, it pushes up its slender culms, no more than an inch and a half in diameter, so rapidly as to suppress all competing shrubs and undergrowth, and forms dense thickets that are further compressed by the pressure of heavy snowfalls which weigh down its feathery tips and freeze them to the ground. In these thickets visibility may be no more than from two to thirty feet, and a man can force his way through them only with the greatest difficulty.

It was in these bamboo jungles that Chi-Chi and An-An were born, and in them have been born all but two or three of the world's entire stock of giant pandas during the past million or more years. Nature has provided few animals with such an impregnable sanctuary. And, what is more, most pandas rarely have cause to venture outside this sanctuary, because within it they live literally surrounded by an inexhaustible supply of their staple food, the bamboo-culms – enough bamboo to keep every giant panda fully fed throughout the twenty-five or thirty years of his comfortable lifespan.

But if the giant panda, together with the snub-nosed monkey, the musk deer and the takin, prefers the cold climate of the high bamboo jungles and conifer forests, the mountain ranges that run from north to south create a barrier against the westerly winds, ensuring plentiful rains for deciduous forest growth, and the deep, grassy valleys are warm and fertile during the summer months. In some valleys buckwheat, oats, beans, peas and barley are cultivated to a height of thirteen thousand feet up the hillsides, while wild flowers grow luxuriantly in the deep ravines. And in the woods above the cultivated fields are spruces, junipers, yews and cypresses, poplars, horse-chestnuts and wild cherries, alders and the evergreen prickly oak, though these woods had already been extensively denuded by charcoal-burners and potash-makers a hundred years ago. Their camps are still everywhere in the forests, and the game show no fear of their fires or the perpetual smoke from these.

As late in the season as June, however, snow and frost may cut the blooms of the flowers in the valleys; and that heavy cloud, torrential rains and dense mists perennially shroud the hills and valleys of Hsi-fan is inherent in the name of Yunnan – 'South of the Cloud'. On 12 June Père David noted that: 'The rain, heavier than usual, has swollen the streams, which are carrying away most of the bridges made of treetrunks. From my room, where my illness keeps me, I hear the continual noise of landslides, which ruin fields in the valleys. Stones and rocks roll and bound noisily, breaking everything in their way. I am told that this happens every year after such a storm. The devastation is terrible.'

So too another missionary, W. N. Fergusson, describes how,

one day in the middle of May some forty years later, he was eating his lunch on the crest of one of the ridges above Wenchuan, at the junction of the Min and Chengou rivers some seventy-five miles to the north-east of Muping, when: 'After a tremendous struggle up the precipitous cliffs, dragging ourselves up by catching hold of the brushwood and scrub bamboo, there suddenly came a great crash and roar as if the earth had split in two, and even the hunters looked aghast; but it was only a landslide, and part of one of the mountains was seen sliding down into the valley, whose slopes were dotted with the dull grey stone dwellings of the Wassu and Changming peasantry, and the great towers, erected in the villages, that looked like church spires in the distance.'

Above the bamboo jungle, at altitudes of between seven and ten thousand feet, are the rhododendrons – Hsi-fan's glory. 'The gorgeous beauty of their flowers defies description,' wrote the botanist E. H. Wilson one July:

> They were in thousands and hundreds of thousands. Bushes of all sizes, many thirty feet tall and more in diameter, all clad with a wealth of blossoms that almost hid the foliage. Some flowers were crimson, some bright red, some flesh-coloured, some silvery-pink, some yellow, and others pure white. The huge rugged stems were gnarled and twisted into every conceivable shape, and draped with pendant mosses and lichens. How they find roothold on these wild crags and cliffs is a marvel. Many grow on the fallen trunks of the silver fir and some are epiphytic. Beneath them sphagnum moss luxuriates. On bare exposed cliffs I gathered two diminutive species, each only a few inches tall, one with deep purple and the other with pale yellow flowers.

Still higher are the hardy tree-rhododendrons, maintaining life up to heights of sixteen or seventeen thousand feet, two or three thousand feet above the upper limit of the vast primeval forests of fir and pine that made Edward Amundsen homesick for Norway. And between the timber-line and the permanent snow are the great alpine meadows where the large yellow poppies bloom (though every hair on every petal is encased in ice) and bow before the searing winds that sweep down from the eternal

7

snows of the ultimate crags and ridges and peaks. These grasslands, to which the giant panda is not, as we shall see, altogether
a stranger, are the home of Tibetan gazelles, of herds of hundreds
of wild asses and of the giant blue sheep. *Panyang* to the Chinese,
bhural or *bharal* to the big-game hunters of India, the blue sheep
graze in flocks of up to eighty or a hundred, wherever rocky
ground affords cover for a sentinel to stand on watch over the
open, rolling downs of steppes and low hills – miles and miles of
blue and brown hills – that stretch away as far as his eye can
see in the clear light, with here and there an encampment of
Tibetan herdsmen.

The giant panda himself needs no describing. So with this
introduction we can now turn to the few on-the-spot reports of the
giant panda in his bamboo jungle. To continue using his double-
barrelled name would, however, be most tiresome, and might also
lead to confusion with the lesser panda, which ranges through the
Himalayan forests at altitudes of between 7,000 and 13,000 feet
from Nepal eastwards, and less commonly as a larger and more
thickly furred race in Szechwan, Yunnan, northern Burma and
Laos. Known to the Chinese as *Ho-hu* or *Hun-ho*, 'the fire-fox',
because of its fiery-red coat and foxy face and brush, and to the
hill peoples of the Himalayas and Hsi-fan by a variety of other
names, this little panda is not much more than three feet in length,
including its long and bushy ringed tail, and weighs no more than
eight or ten pounds. For the past one hundred and fifty years this
is the animal that has been known in the West (though nowhere
in the East) as the panda – a name that may be a Western corruption of the Nepali word *nigalya-ponya*, 'eater of bamboo'. For
centuries Chinese pictures and manuscripts, history-books,
children's books and tax-rolls are said to have referred to the
giant panda as *Peihsiung*, 'the white bear'. The colloquial *beishung*
will serve our purpose hereafter.

CHAPTER TWO

Ancient History

It was on the night of 27 or 28 February that Père David had arrived in Muping, some four and a half months after setting out on the second of the three major explorations of China that he undertook between the years 1862 and 1874. In those days an expedition into the barbarous land of Hsi-fan involved six weeks' sailing and portage up the Yangtze to Chungking, followed by the long slog up hill and down dale and over high mountain passes to the ancient walled town of Chengtu, capital of Szechwan. If he arrived safely in Chengtu, the weary traveller had then to suffer

9

further protracted mortification of the flesh over Szechwan's causeways, only four feet in width and 'paved with good intentions and solid flagstones, which latter must in many instances be centuries or tens of centuries old'. With a surveyor's outraged sense of propriety at the nature of Chinese roads through the ages, R. L. Jack added that:

> The wear of ironshod hoofs has rounded the flagstones into smooth boulders and widened the intervening spaces until it becomes a mere chance whether the traveller steps on a boulder or into the mud; or, where it happens that the middle of a flagstone in some far-off time offered the best foothold, the successive impact of hoofs in the same spot has drilled a hole right through the stone into the mud beneath. Men and animals stagger, slip, and flounder over these pavements, which are frequently left, by the progress of denudation, standing on ridges of earth. The farmer does not scruple to acquire soil for top-dressing by paring the road away or by undermining it, and even throws a dam across it, whenever he sees fit, to convert it into a reservoir for the irrigation of his rice-field. The road must go round, never through, a rice-field, and nothing is more common than to see a road which ought to be straight going round three sides of a square. An ascent is always negotiated by flights of steps.

Père David does not say whether he trekked the one hundred miles or so from Chengtu to Muping on foot, or whether he allowed himself to be trundled along in the ubiquitous wheel-barrow or carried in a *wha-gar*, the Chinese equivalent of a sedan chair, comprising a cradle slung on two long bamboo poles with a swing below for the occupant's feet. But although he was no longer a fit man he did not allow the ordeal of his journey to interfere with his scientific observations. Within days of his settling in at the college he was noting in his diary for 11 March that:

> On returning from an excursion we are invited to rest at the home of a certain Li, the principal land-owner in the valley, who serves us tea and sweetmeats. At this pagan's I see a fine

skin of the famous white and black bear, which appears to be fairly large. It is a remarkable species and I am delighted to hear my hunters say that I shall certainly obtain the animal within a short time. They tell me they will go out tomorrow to kill this animal, which will surely provide an interesting novelty for science.

Now, this entry was made only eleven days after Père David's arrival in Muping, and yet he refers to 'the famous white and black bear' as if its existence was a byword throughout China and common knowledge among his brother missionaries. Since a Lazarist college had been founded in Muping almost fifty years earlier by missionaries seeking sanctuary, in this independent princedom of the Mantzu, from persecution in China proper, it is reasonable to assume that its pastors were indeed aware of the unique particoloured 'bear' that lived in the bamboo jungles above Muping, though probably not acquainted with the living animal as the beishung seldom approached human habitation except when raiding the peasants' beehives.

Ten days later David was writing to Professor Alphonse Milne-Edwards, the eminent French zoologist, in Paris: 'I have worked well these first three weeks and I have made a good number of hunts after the animals which inhabit these forests. As it will not be possible for my collection to arrive in Paris for a very long time, I pray that you will publish immediately the following summary description of a bear which seems to me to be new to science. I have never seen this specimen in European cabinets, which is the prettiest kind I know.'

And in his diary for the 23rd he expresses the view that: 'This must be a new specimen of *Ursus*, very remarkable not only because of its colour, but also for its paws, which are hairy underneath.'

His letter to Milne-Edwards included a brief description of a young beishung which his hunters had captured alive two days earlier (on 23 March, according to his diary) but had killed so that they could carry it more easily. He also mentions that he had seen some mutilated skins of full-grown beishung, and that for twenty days previously he had employed more than ten hunters to capture specimens of this 'remarkable bear'.

Portrait of Chi-Chi, showing the forward-growing fur on the muzzle which
beishung have in common with bears. *(Zoological Society of London)*

Now, again, I do not believe that any naturalist, let alone one devoting considerable time to religious duties, would within twenty-four hours of settling into his new habitat organize hunting-parties for a previously unknown animal and within the next three weeks obtain specimens, pen descriptions of them, and pack off a skin to Europe, *unless* he had been in previous possession of information concerning it, or had at least suspected that some such animal existed. I do not believe, further, that a naturalist who had made as many expeditions throughout the length and breadth of China as David had done during the previous seven years, and who was continually inquiring about the local fauna and flora (with the same insatiable curiosity that distinguished Gilbert White of Selborne), would not have heard very soon after his arrival in China of the famous white and black bear.

In fact David had known for some time that the Director of the college, M. Arnal, had for two years been making a collection of the birds and mammals of Hsi-fan; and before he set out from Shanghai a former Chinese pupil of the college had told him that Arnal's hunters had not succeeded in procuring all the animals in the woods around Muping. 'So,' commented David, 'there will still be some gleanings for me, at least among the less remarkable species.'

With the true naturalist's scepticism, David did not allow himself to be carried away by extravagant hopes, and before leaving Chengtu on the last stage of his journey to unknown Hsi-fan he wrote in his diary: 'I am busy preparing my numerous pieces of baggage to leave tomorrow and, if it please God, spend a year in Muping, the promised land where everyone has said there are marvels. I admit, however, that I am not enthusiastic, knowing how often I have been misled by Chinese promises.'

The Chinese have been aware of the existence of giant pandas in Hsi-fan for a very long time – as they have also of that of the unique snow-monkey. Indeed, if one of their chronicles, the *Tribute of Yu*, has been translated correctly, an emperor of that name was receiving the *P'i* or panda as a part of his tribute more than four thousand years ago from the inhabitants of Liangchow, which was rich in 'bears, pandas and foxes' and was not more than two hundred miles north of the beishung's present known range. Possibly *Pei-hsiung* is in fact a corruption of *P'i;* but on the other hand the reference is ambiguous and could be taken as applicable to the little red panda. Again, according to the *Chi-King* (the Sacred Book of Songs), Wu-Wang, progenitor of the Chou dynasty, caused to be built in 1050 BC a Park of Intelligence, in which his successors kept, among other animals, giant pandas, tigers and rhinoceroses. Another chronicle, compiled in AD 621, during the reign of the first of the T'ang emperors, refers to a white bear inhabiting the bamboo forests in the mountains of Yunnan; and later that century the Japanese Imperial Annals record that on 22 October 685 the Emperor of China dispatched to the Tenno of Japan a gift of two live white bears, together with seventy white bearskins.

A thousand years after this the aboriginal peoples of western Szechwan and eastern Tibet were paying tribute in beishung skins to the Mantzu princelings. The Chinese did not actually invade the Mantzus' territories in Hsi-fan until the middle of the nineteenth century, but one of the great silk-routes from China to central Asia and Europe had passed through the heart of the beishung's country for more than seventeen centuries. It is thus reasonable to assume that skins of the beishung, and no doubt live specimens also, must have been offered from time to time to the merchants and carriers traversing Hsi-fan. For centuries Tatsienlu, 'the Forge of the Arrows', lying more than 8,000 feet above sea-level in its verdant green valley some fifty miles south-west of Muping, was the great trading-mart of eastern Tibet. Through it furs, hides and wool, gold-dust, musk and deer's antlers were exported to China, while immense quantities of tea-bricks were imported to Tibet from Yachow in western Szech-wan, where tea was grown on all the surrounding hillsides. As recently as the early years of this century no less than fourteen and a half million pounds of bricks were being imported annually on the backs of coolies, each carrying a staggering load of up to 360 pounds; but the most extraordinary goods transported by these carriers, over the ten-thousand-foot snow-covered passes between the Ningyuenfu Valley and Chengtu, were live parrots perched on wooden frames, a hundred or more to a frame.

Despite this centuries-old awareness in China of the existence in the savage border marches of Hsi-fan of a unique kind of white bear, and despite these equally ancient overland trade-routes between China and the West, it has always been supposed that not even a rumour of the beishung had reached the West before David's time. I would deem it much more probable that when that sly fox Milne-Edwards, impressed by David's exceptional skill as a naturalist, arranged with the Jesuits to have him transferred from Italy to the Lazarist mission at Peking in 1862, his chief hopes were not only that David would be able to send back to the Jardin des Plantes in Paris extensive collections of China's flora and fauna, which were almost unknown in the West, but that these collections might include the mysterious white bear and other fabulous creatures inhabiting the Sino-Tibetan borderlands. As it happened, Milne-Edwards could not have selected a better man for the job, for David had been a naturalist from his boyhood days and had also set his heart on missionary work in China as far back as 1851, when, at the age of twenty-five, he had become a member of the Mission of St Vincent de Paul, whose priests were known as Lazarists; and this hardy, self-sufficient Basque from the hill-country of the Basses-Pyrénées must have succeeded beyond Milne-Edwards's wildest dreams, for even today the Jardin des Plantes claims to have the most comprehensive collection of Chinese animals and plants of any Western museum – the bulk of them collected by David.

A flowering peach, a clematis, a buddleia and a lily are all named after this indefatigable naturalist, though he is most widely known for the strange deer that bear his name. His discovery of these was typical of the man. From the time of his arrival in Peking he had been curious to know what animals inhabited the Imperial Hunting Park, situated a couple of miles outside the city. Although the park included several villages it was encircled by a high wall some twelve leagues in circumference and was forbidden territory to Europeans – and to most Chinese, for that matter. Père David often walked beside the wall, in the hope that he might chance to find a gate open or a breach in the wall through which he might view the park, but it was not until a September morning in 1865 that such an opportunity occurred, when he came upon a large heap of sand deposited by workmen repairing the wall. This enabled him to clamber onto the top of the wall, and what he saw he described in a letter to Milne-Edwards. 'I was fortunate enough to see a herd of more than a hundred animals which looked to me like Elks. Unfortunately they carried no antlers at this time; what distinguishes the animal I have seen is the length of its tail, which appeared to be relatively as long as that of the donkey, a feature not to be found in any of the deer known to me. It is also smaller than the northern Elk.'

After making some discreet inquiries about this strange deer, Père David wrote further to Milne-Edwards that:

> I have made unsuccessful attempts to obtain the skin of this species. It is impossible even to secure scraps of it, and the French Legation feel unable to procure this curious animal by unofficial approaches to the Chinese Government. Fortunately I know some of the Tartar soldiers who do guard-duty in the Park, and I am sure that, by means of a bribe, I shall obtain some skins which I shall hasten to send to you. The Chinese call this animal *Mi-lou* or, more often, *Sseupou-siang*, which indicates the four features that distinguish it; because they consider that this deer resembles the stag with its antlers, the cow with its hooves, the camel with its neck and the mule or even the donkey with its tail.

It must be said that Père David's trafficking with the guards was distinctly un-Christian! However, on the night of 30 January the following year, after he had made payment to the guards of twenty taels in two portions (since neither party apparently trusted the other!), the hides and bones of a male and a female *Mi-lou* were dropped over the wall to David; and these he was able to forward to Milne-Edwards. During the next four years the Chinese Government surprisingly supplied David with a number of live *Mi-lou*, which he was able to ship to various European zoos. He could not have known that the herd of *Mi-lou* in the Park was the only one in China, still less suspected that he was saving a species from total extinction. But it was so: for by 1900, after floods had breached the wall and the herd had escaped to the outside world, to be decimated by the peasantry and finally exterminated by foreign troops during the Boxer rising, the stock bred from those he had sent to Europe were the sole survivors of their race. Despite many vicissitudes these prospered, and the wheel of chance turned full circle when, in

Père David's Deer. *(Zoological Society of London)*

1957, the Zoological Society of London was able to export four young Père David's deer to Peking, with a view to re-establishing this unique marsh deer in its native habitat.

But to return to Père David in Szechwan in 1869. He was certainly an energetic organizer, for on 1 April, only eleven days after he wrote his first letter from Muping, his Christian hunters brought him two live beishung, one of which was an adult female. As there are no further references to these, they presumably died or were killed; though Helen Fox, in her abridged translation of

An-An at Moscow Zoo. (*Zoological Society of London*)

David's diaries, commented: 'It can be imagined what a stir was caused when a panda arrived at the Jardin d'Acclimatation. For a while it was the only example in Europe; but the first to come did not long survive its transference from the mountains of Szechwan.' However, there is no confirmation in any other quarter of live beishung reaching Europe during the nineteenth century, though there is a persistent tradition that they did, and even that 'in 1888 the Jardin des Plantes had four Giant Pandas, the only examples outside China' – procured by Père David. But there is no mention of these in his *La Faune chinoise*, published in 1889; and Helen Fox and others may have been confused by the fact that the first live lesser red panda to be seen in the West did, curiously enough, arrive in London from the western Himalayas late in May 1869. It would in any case have been virtually impossible at that time for a giant panda, a bamboo-eater, to have survived the long overland journey of several months from Hsi-fan to Shanghai and the still longer subsequent voyage by sea.

To Père David's brief notes on the beishung we shall have occasion to refer in due course, for forty-five years were to pass before a live beishung was definitely seen by another Westerner. To a naturalist so fanatically curious as David it must have been a bitter disappointment not to have added the giant panda to those other rare mammals of China and Mongolia he had seen in the wild state, and for us it is a tragedy that he was unable to make any personal observations of wild beishung. But he who had withstood the sandstorms of the Mongolian steppes and the hardships of seven years' almost continual travelling found the rugged country of *Ngam-grog-chi* too rigorous after years of constant privation. Within a few weeks of his arrival at Muping David was too ill to undertake any fieldwork of an arduous nature, although he remained at the college until late in November and did not finally return to France until 1874.

CHAPTER THREE

Hunting Him - Western Style

If Père David did not send back a live beishung to the Jardin d'Acclimatation he did deposit four skins in the Museum; but his description of his new bear, published in the *Nouvelles Archives* in 1872, did not lead to the immediate discovery of more beishung by Western explorers, plant-collectors and big-game hunters, although a skin turned up in Stuttgart some ten years later from an unknown source. It was indeed the end of the century before any further reports of beishung were received in the West. These came from a Russian explorer, M. M. Berezovski, who, when exploring the Tsingling Shan on the border between Szechwan and Kansu in the years 1884-7, saw skins of beishung collected by native hunters. But, since these reports came from a region three hundred miles to the north-east of the beishung's most northerly recognized haunts in the Wassu country around Wen-chuan, they were apparently ignored for the next fifty years or so, despite the fact that Berezovski brought home several skins with him.

However, in 1896, hunters employed by F. W. Styan killed a beishung in the Yangliupa district of north-western Szechwan. Then between 1898 and 1910 Wilson the botanist, travelling widely throughout Hsi-fan, sometimes accompanied by W. R. Zappey, collected some information on the beishung's habits and distribution from the natives, and found traces of them himself in the country around Tatsienlu and also at Wa Shan, some eighty miles to the south-east; while in 1903 the missionary J. H. Edgar, when travelling on the upper Tung river due west of Muping, reported that the inhabitants of Takin had told him of an unusual animal which they classed with the bears. Thirteen years later, when he was on an expedition with the explorer General G. E. Pereira through the wild and densely forested Kin Sha country, and was about midway between Batang and Dzeng (or Dzerge), some 175 miles — and three weeks' hard travelling — west of Tatsienlu, Edgar saw an animal asleep in the fork of a high tree. He noted that it was '. . . very large, seemed quite white, and was curled up in a great ball very much after the manner of the cats. It was unknown, and a source of wonder to my Tibetans. As I was unarmed I did not approach nearer than one hundred yards, and a fierce thunderstorm finally sent us hurrying to a farmhouse near the limit of settled population.'

Since this animal was unknown to his Tibetan followers, it is more likely to have been a beishung than a brown bear, with which they would have been well acquainted. However, indivi-duals of one local race of the brown bear are reported to be so light a shade of brown as to be almost a silvery white in colour, with creamy underfur, and are known to have been mistaken for beishung by travellers and hunters. No two authorities appear to agree on the status and distribution of the various races of bears in Hsi-fan, but it would appear that there is also a black form of the brown bear, which has a broad white band across the chest and extended upwards in front of the shoulders to form a yoke round the neck, though this is the normal insignia of a black bear. This bear, known to the Chinese as *Ma-hsiung*, 'the horse-bear', is greatly feared by the Tibetans as *Dry-mu*, 'the Devil's grand-mother'. It appears to be mainly an inhabitant of the steppe, and there is some doubt as to whether these various brown bears enter the bamboo jungle. They are certainly less numerous than the Asiatic black bears and the Tibetan blue bears, both of which are to be found at all heights in the forests. The latter, another race of the brown bear, might also perhaps be confused with a beishung, with its very pale blond fur (which can be mixed with black hairs, imparting a bluish tinge to its coat) and its black dorsal stripe.

In the meantime a German zoologist, Hugo Weigold, had become the first Westerner since David indisputably to see a live beishung. In 1914, when he was in the country east of the Chengou river, a cub was brought to him by his Wassu hunters, descendants of tribesmen brought in from south-western Tibet by the Chinese almost a thousand years earlier to assist them in conquering the native Changming; but as the cub was a suckling only a few days old he was unable to procure suitable food for it, and it soon died. On a second expedition to this region two years later Weigold was again unable to obtain a live beishung, though he tracked one for several days through the bamboo; but he did purchase half a dozen skins that eventually found their way to a Berlin museum.

This was the period of the First World War, and Weigold's 'rediscovery' of the beishung did not become generally known until some twenty years later. Only nine Westerners have certainly seen a live beishung in the wild state; and Weigold, who is now over eighty years of age, recently recalled his memories of beishung with affection on the BBC's *Look* programme.

By 1928 more than half a century had passed since David had introduced the beishung to the outside world, and still no Westerner had come face to face with a wild beishung in a bamboo jungle. But in the autumn of that year Theodore and Kermit Roosevelt set out on an expedition, sponsored by the Field Museum of Chicago, to Indo-China and Hsi-fan. They were accompanied by Suydam Cutting, the Tibetan explorer, and by J. T. Young, a Honolulu-born Chinese hunter, as interpreter. After landing at Rangoon they made their way up the Irrawaddy, and then with mule transport up the old Burma–Yunnan trail from Bhamo to Talifu and north-eastwards by way of Likiang and Bedung, through country infested with bandits and independent-minded Lo-Lo aboriginals on the western marches of the beishung's range. It was midwinter and very cold, with snow lying deep in the mountains; for most of the way they were travelling at heights of between ten and fourteen thousand feet, and above seventeen thousand when crossing passes.

At every halt the Roosevelts interrogated the Lo-Los and the local Chinese officials as to the presence of beishung in their country. But it was not until early in March that they found the first definite traces of them, in the neighbourhood of Muping. They hunted through the bamboo jungle for ten days with half a dozen of the local hunters and their small, wiry black and tan dogs, and located numbers of beishung tracks, but that was their only reward. The dogs had poor noses and the jungle was dense, permitting a maximum field of view of only twenty or thirty feet. Experienced explorers though they were, the Roosevelts had never encountered such jungle. Scrub bamboo, six or eight feet in height, was interspersed with hemlock and beech on slopes inclined at forty-five degrees, up which they had to climb on hands and knees. 'Deadfall blocked us every few feet. The dust from the dried bamboo leaves got into our lungs and eyes. The stems and matted vines through which we had to force our way tripped and clung to us like the tentacles of an octopus.'

After this unsuccessful hunt in the country around Muping they turned south, bound for Indo-China; but although they found moderately fresh tracks of beishung in an even denser jungle at Luchinga, that was all. On 6 April, when three hours out from Tsalo in its fertile valley among the hillside fields of maize and wheat and opium poppies, they were met by a hunter with the news that a peasant had approached him for the loan of a rifle with which to protect the village beehives from the raids of a beishung which, after being wounded on a previous visit to the hives a month earlier, had now returned to them. But again the Roosevelts were out of luck, and for another week they trekked on

23

A study of An-An giving an accurate idea of the massive solidity of the adult male beishung. (*Zoological Society of London*)

south down the valleys through the mountains, whose slopes were sprinkled with small blue orchids and blue lilies, forget-me-nots and primulas, and glorious with rhododendron blooms of the deepest purple, white and, especially, pink. But signs of beishung were much scarcer here than around Muping; and on 12 April, after passing down a wide grassy valley, hemmed in by well-forested hills of great pines, vast alpine meadows and snow-clad peaks, they reached the group of hamlets known as Yehli, almost a hundred miles south-east of Tatsienlu. Heavy rain and dense fog shrouded the valley.

Early next morning snow lay in the valley and over the forests; but a thin, misty rain was falling when the party set out in search of beishung once more, guided by four Lo-Lo hunters with five lean black dogs. In a ravine seven or eight miles up the valley they came across tracks in the snow. These were four or five hours old and had been made by a beishung moving leisurely from one thicket to another, browsing on the bamboos. Then for a mile or more a boar's tracks were superimposed on those of the beishung, which followed the rocky bed of an old watercourse before climbing a steep slope through a maze of deadfall trunks, slippery with snow and ice. After upwards of three hours of this hard going they ultimately broke through into less dense jungle, where lichenous alders and tall spruces towered above the bamboo; and here at the root of a tree they stumbled on a beishung's resting-place, formed of bamboo-stalks twisted into a kind of nest. Hairs adhering to the twigs and branches suggested that the nest had been fashioned by the beishung turning round and round as a dog does. When they were examining the claw-marks that scored the bark of the tree, and the tracks that led in all directions, their attention was attracted by a clicking chirp that could have been the snapping of a bamboo or the creaking of the interlocked branches of two swaying trees. But the Lo-Los knew better, and after running forwards for some forty yards one of the hunters pointed to a giant spruce thirty yards from him. From its hollow bole were emerging the head and forequarters of an adult

24

beishung. When it had extricated itself, while gazing sleepily from side to side, this male beishung appeared unexpectedly large to the Roosevelts, its size accentuated by its dramatic parti-colouring — the broad white head with its pronounced black spectacles, the heavy black collar and white saddle. As it walked slowly away into the bamboos it was fired on simultaneously by the brothers and hit by both bullets. This caused it to flounder through deep snow, drifted into a hollow, to within five or six feet of them; but, making a temporary recovery, it turned away through the bamboo and covered seventy-five yards before finally succumbing.

The Roosevelts' success in actually killing a beishung, and in procuring half a dozen skins from the natives, inevitably sparked off a series of field expeditions financed by museums and zoo-logical gardens avid for skins and specimens of the no longer semi-mythical giant panda. As early as the following summer of 1930 the aptly named man on the spot, Dr David Crockett Graham of the West China Union University, at Chengtu on the eastern marches of the beishung's country, set off for Muping with some of the Roosevelts' hunters; but though he purchased a skin from a local hunter and saw numbers of tracks no live beishung were forthcoming for slaughter. In that year also a young American, Brooke Dolan, was leading a two-year expedi-tion into Hsi-fan for the Philadelphia Academy of Natural Sciences. Among the members of this expedition was a German zoologist, Ernst Schäfer, who on 13 May 1931 shot a second giant panda, a young female, on a hillside near Chengwai in the Wassu country. For this crime he made some amends by publishing notes of the beishung's habits.

The following year Jack Young either shot or obtained a third beishung, an adult, to the north of Tatsienlu; and in 1934 the American Musuem of Natural History dispatched two more collectors, Dean Sage and William Sheldon, in quest of beishung specimens for its show-cases. Early in September that year these two reached the hamlet of Tsao-Po in the foothills of the Wassu country to the east of the Min river, after two days' motoring up the bad road between Chungking and Chengtu and a further week's footslogging over the two hundred miles into beishung country. *En route* they had run into a colourful character, Floyd

Tangier Smith (a fifty-year-old ex-banker familiarly known as
'Ajax' Smith in Shanghai, where he lived when not on animal-
collecting expeditions), who was also collecting for a rival body —
the Chicago Field Museum — and whom we shall meet again.

Initially Sage and Sheldon camped at 10,000 feet in the Chen
Liang Shan, with the intention of collecting *bharal*, specimens of
which were also required for the museum's showcases. But
though they lay out for hours at a time within earshot of ledges
on the cliffs, 'where the tinkle of dislodged rocks told us that
sheep were feeding or resting', and saw in all upwards of a
hundred blue sheep, the perpetual fog prevented them from
obtaining more than four specimens. So in the middle of October
they made their way north-west into the beautiful valleys of Mao
Mo Gu and Chengwai, and concentrated their search for beishung on a forty-mile quarter-circle some ten miles to the south
of Wenchuan. At a farmhouse in the Chengwai valley, where
Schäfer had obtained his beishung, they were shown the skins
of two that had been taken in spear-traps.

Although an occasional beishung was shot in a tree by a farmer's
old muzzle-loader, the few skins to be seen in Hsi-fan houses
were mainly those of beishung that had been 'accidentally' killed
in these spear-traps, which were traditionally used by hunters
and woodcutters for any large game — as they were in Africa. In
Hsi-fan the trap comprised a bamboo fence about thirty inches
in height laid across a game-trail, with a gap where the fence cut
the track. An iron-headed spear, or a pole with a sharp knife
attached, was laid horizontally between two upright sticks at one
side of the gap and attached by its shaft to a bent sapling operated
by a trip-cord. If an animal's foot or leg touched the cord, the
sapling was sprung by means of a trigger and the spear driven
across the track with tremendous impetus into the animal's body
behind the shoulder. Since the traps might be left in position
from one year to the next, often without their knives or spear-
heads being removed, they constituted a hazard to explorers and
beishung-hunters and even to the natives themselves, for one of
Fergusson's guides showed him a scar where a knife had been
sprung right through one thigh and into the other.

Encouraged by their experience at the Chengwai farmhouse
Sage and Sheldon climbed the bamboo-clad ridges above the two

valleys day after day, '. . . thrashing through bamboo jungles of unbelievable intensity, and as winter came on us, wading through snow and creeping over ice-covered ledges. From the very beginning we found panda signs – chewed ends of bamboo and droppings. Some very old; others quite fresh. We set spear-traps; we searched acres and acres of bamboo-covered slopes with our fieldglasses. We hunted with dogs. Unreliable curs that would run anything from a deer to a pheasant.'

The local hunters brought in another beishung skin among those of black bears, boars, goral, serow and takin, and their dogs drove three separate beishung out of bamboo thickets, but though following these closely Sage and Sheldon were not able to get a shot at any of them. On 8 December, therefore, they set out from Chengwai for the bamboo jungles determined to make a last effort to obtain a beishung with the aid of all the dogs they could muster. Sage's account of the events of that day, as set down in his journal, was subsequently published in the *China Journal*.

We started up a tributary valley with the intention of hunting the same slope which Kan, the native tracker, had worked with his dogs yesterday. Our reason for choosing this spot was that it was new ground and we knew from the tracks seen on the river bar that *Beishung* had been there recently, so that it offered at least as good a chance as anywhere, and possibly better. It was a beautiful morning, clear and cold.

An hour's ride brought us to the old tracks, and we turned up the ridge following Kan's route of yesterday. We climbed steadily upwards for an hour and a half, encountering the habitual cliffs and bamboo. There is no such thing as horizontal hunting in Wassu: it is all vertical. We crossed one old Panda track in the snow. At 11 o'clock we came to some open ledges and sat down for a bite to eat and a look with the glasses. The dogs were very restless and kept whining and testing the wind. We thought they might have detected the presence of Takin, one or two of which – to judge from the tracks – had passed here yesterday.

Ascending from the ledges, we began to swing in a general north-easterly direction along the ridge, Kan leading the way. We soon found the two- or three-day-old trail of a *Beishung* and began to follow it. The going was very difficult, being principally through patches of bamboo and over ledges. The side of the ridge was cut by frequent ravines and gullies, some being quite wide. On the northern slopes of the ravines there was a good deal of snow, certainly six to eight inches, and possibly more, and here tracking was ideal. But on those which had a southern exposure, the snow had been completely melted off, and following the track was not so easy. Several times we lost it, but always picked it up again. There was a pretty good route of chewed bamboos and droppings to show where the animal had travelled along, and we found two places where it had rested. One was at the foot of a big spruce tree. The snow was packed down hard, and there was a great quantity of droppings. The other spot was on a ledge in the sun. The droppings we found were all composed of bamboo stalks, with not a leaf among them.

We worked along the ridge for about two hours, and then stopped to rest for a while on a sunny slope. At this point the pursuit seemed vain and decidely discouraging. The track was unquestionably old, I was inclined to think three or four days, and the dogs showed not the slightest interest. They were still leashed. Curiously enough, as we were sitting there in the sun, we reviewed the shooting of both Schäfer's and the Roosevelts' *Beishungs* and analysed the factors contributing to their success. We both agreed that almost a given set of conditions was necessary for the bagging of one of these animals, and the conditions practically never coincided with the opportunity.

We went on for half an hour more and reached a gully where the snow was quite deep, and the tracks looked depressingly old. The hour was getting on, and there was not much time left to hunt. We decided, as a last measure, to let the dogs go and let them range about for a while. They started along the tracks without much enthusiasm, and we followed. I remember distinctly feeling it was a pretty hopeless chance, and I think the men felt so too, for they kept muttering, '*Beishung mutte, beishung mutte!*' I stopped to examine some old droppings, and Bill and the other hunters got pretty well ahead of Wong and myself, so that they were out of sight. Hurrying to catch up with them, we came out of the snow and climbed a very steep little slope covered with dead leaves. I recall it well, for I used the butt of my rifle as a staff to help me up, and when we topped a ledge looking into a snow-filled bamboo ravine on the other side, I was breathing hard. There was a big spruce tree there, and I leaned my rifle up against it and took off my gloves. I saw Bill moving about a hundred yards above me and called out to him, 'Oh! Bill, what do you see?' He replied, 'Nothing, but the men have gone up this way; they're following the dogs.' Just then there came the sound of a faint and distant bark. Bill said, 'There go the dogs now,' and I called back, 'Yes, but they're way down below us.' It was true, for the sound came up the snow-filled ravine on the edge of which we stood. All of a sudden I heard the unmistakable noise of breaking bamboos, and the barking became louder. Wong said, '*Beishung!*'

Now at this moment it never occurred to me that we would ever see the animal. If, indeed, the dogs had started one out, the chances were he would go crashing off into the bamboos and that would be the end of it. Nevertheless, I took my gun and tried to put a cartridge into the chamber. It was all covered with snow and ice from the recent hard going, and the shell would not go in, so I threw it away – an act which was later to become of the greatest importance – and put in another one. Above me Bill began to climb rapidly to gain a better vantage-point, but I was in an ideal spot and did not move. Up the ravine came the dogs, their barking growing steadily louder, and the bamboos crackling at a great rate. Suddenly, I heard the deep angry growl of a large animal, and I began to get really excited. And then – as if in a dream – I saw a giant panda coming through the bamboos about 60 yards away from me. He was heading straight up the ravine with the dogs at his heels. I fired and heard the bullet strike. I yelled, 'I've got him.' The panda made a right-angled turn and came straight for the ledge I was standing on, not running – walking rapidly is the only way to describe it. His head hung low and swayed from side to side. His tongue was out, and he was panting. He appeared to be looking at the ground, and apparently did not see me at all. I frantically worked the bolt of my rifle and snapped the hammer on an empty chamber. In a daze, thoughts flashed through my mind: no more bullets. What'll I do? He's only 20 feet away, now 15 feet. He's coming straight at me. Can I kill him with the butt of the rifle? I felt a cartridge thrust into my hand by Wong. It was the discarded one which he had picked up. I jammed it in the gun and fired into the *Beishung's* fur. He was less than ten feet from me!

At the same instant Bill shot from above. Down the slope he rolled, over and over, and came to a stop against a tree fifty yards below.

It was the most dramatic experience I have ever had. As long as I live I shall never forget the sight of that great animal plunging towards me. I don't believe he ever saw me. I think he was trying to get across the ridge, and I happened to be right square in his path. He appeared very large in size and not at all white, but rather a dirty cream colour. Very conspicuous was the dark fur around the eyes, which gave them a downcast expression. It was the one striking thing that drew my attention. The other black markings I never noticed at all.

The animal's stride was curious. I got the impression he was badly bothered by the dogs and was rather bewildered. I think he was moving as rapidly as he was capable of, and yet he was only going at a fast walk. I am sure he was walking flat-footed and not bending his paws under as a bear does, for the stride was quite stiff-legged and altogether lacking in suppleness.

When we came to examine the creature, we found it to be a large old female that looked as if she had been nursing. She measured just about 5 feet, from tip to tip.

It was 2.30 when we shot her, and four o'clock when the skin was finally rolled up and we started for camp. The descent of the mountain was an ordeal. We went right down the gully that the Panda had come up, through quite deep snow, slipping, sliding and falling through bamboos and over stones and logs. The lower part of the slope was all bamboo cliffs, and almost all hunting in this country is attended by some danger, because of the constant cliff climbing and the risk of falling on one of the sharp bamboo stumps which stick up out of the ground like spearpoints.

For the death of beishung number four Sage and Sheldon also made some amends by adding considerably to our knowledge of

The lumbering, pigeon-toed walk which is the beishung's only means of locomotion.
(*Tierbilder Okapia, Frankfurt*)

its habits. Not so Captain Courtney Brocklehurst, a former game-warden in the Sudan, who shot number five in the same jungles in April of the following year. His failure to publish any detailed notes on his exploit is particularly regrettable because the animal he shot was the male of a pair.

CHAPTER FOUR

Bringing 'em Back Alive

The year 1936 brought an entirely new type of beishung-collector to China, and one whom no novelist in his most imaginative mood could have assigned to such a quest.

A year or two earlier W. H. Harkness, the 'bring-'em-back-alive' collector of Komodo dragons from Indonesia, had been commissioned by the New York Bronx Zoo to procure a live beishung for them. After ten months of negotiations with the Chinese authorities Harkness finally obtained their permission to enter western China with an expedition, one of whose members

34

was reported to be Jack Young and another, inevitably, Tangier Smith, who had just returned from leading another American expedition into Hsi-fan. Nevertheless the party was turned back at Kiating, on the grounds that Szechwan was 'politically unstable', and in February 1936 Harkness died in Shanghai.

On receiving the news of his death his young widow, a New York clothes-designer, determined to mount her own expedition, with the intention not of shooting a beishung but of bringing one home alive, although she lacked any experience of animals or exploring. With this revolutionary end in view Ruth Harkness sailed from the United States in April. She travelled on slow boats and it was July before she finally arrived in China, still at a complete loss as to how to set about capturing a wild beishung. Eventually, however, she contacted Quentin Young, Jack's twenty-year-old brother, who had also had previous experience of beishung-hunting.

Her original intention had been to trap and bring back alive an adult beishung. But on learning from Quentin that a full-grown beishung was a massive beast, as large as an American black bear, she wisely modified this plan, appreciating that the transport of such a large animal from the mountains of Hsi-fan to Shanghai, let alone to New York, would be rather more than she could handle. So they agreed that a beishung cub would be a rather more realistic trophy, and Quentin set out for Hsi-fan, leaving Ruth to sail the fifteen hundred miles up the Yangtze to Chungking in a river-steamer, and thence in a smaller boat up the Ya a further three hundred miles to Kiating, where the Min river joins the Yangtze. This was the (relatively) easy way into Szechwan, if the traveller survived the raging currents and whirlpools in the river's stupendous gorges. At Yachow she joined Quentin for the eight days' trek to Tsao-Po over eleven-thousand-foot passes and ravines spanned by swaying bridges of bamboo cables or merely single strands.

Their luck, or possibly young Quentin's knowledge of the country and skill as a hunter, was phenomenal; for on 9 November, after only ten days' search on the mountains above Tsao-Po, through jungle so dense that they could not see two feet ahead, they put up an adult female beishung. Quentin fired but fortunately missed. Then, in Ruth's words:

35

We plowed on a little further through the dripping bamboo which gradually gave way to a few big trees. Quentin stopped suddenly. He listened for a moment and then went forward so rapidly that I couldn't keep up with him. Dimly I saw him through the wet, waving branches standing near a large rotting tree. I followed as best I could, brushing the water from my face and eyes. Then I, too, stopped – frozen in my tracks.

From the old dead trunk of the tree came a baby's whimper. Quentin reached into the hollow trunk of the tree. Then he turned and walked toward me. In his arms was a baby panda.

Although the cub's eyes were closed, and it was no larger than a kitten, it weighed two or two and a half pounds and can hardly have been less than two weeks old. After a hazardous return journey on their backsides down the craggy slopes through the jungle, with the cub inside Quentin's shirt, they reached camp safely and fed it on dried milk mixed with water. Then, early in November, Ruth set out for America with Su-Lin, as the cub had been named after Jack Young's wife – though it proved subsequently to be a male. They sheltered the first night in a ruined castle, which until the 1911 revolution had been the citadel of a prince of the Wassu, on a high cliff above the Min. The second night they were in an old ruined temple in Wenchuan's walled town; and the three following nights, while still high in the mountains *en route* to Kwanhsien and Chengtu, in small inns roofed with thatch and with bamboo walls and heavy wooden doors.

At Chengtu Quentin parted from Ruth in order to return to Tsao-Po and recover the baggage they had left in camp. According to Ruth it was also his intention to remain in Hsi-fan for some time and study the behaviour of wild beishung. Perhaps he did; but all we know is that he subsequently shot two adults, bringing the toll up to seven in seven years. In the meantime Ruth and Su-Lin had flown to Shanghai and ultimately, after a variety of harrowing experiences which need not concern us here, to America, arriving in San Francisco on 18 December. There Su-Lin was greeted with an appalling ballyhoo, as if he were a unique visitor from outer space, and, after more heartaches – understandably – for his foster-mother, finally lodged in

Chicago's Brookfield Zoo, where he survived until early in the spring of 1938.

By any explorer's or animal-collector's standards, Ruth Harkness's feat in capturing Su-Lin and bringing 'her' back alive was one of extraordinary courage and skill, though in chancing upon a baby beishung only ten days after beginning her search she would appear at first sight to have been outrageously lucky, if we are to believe the reports of local hunters that it often took them several months to capture one. It is not surprising, therefore, that malicious gossip attended her return with Su-Lin: one innuendo being that she had actually acquired the cub, by some feminine subterfuge, from the 'professional' Tangier Smith, since there was circumstantial evidence that he was hunting in the Wassu country at this time. Desmond and Ramona Morris have already examined the controversial pronouncements on Su-Lin's origins in meticulous detail in their book *Men and Pandas,* and they quote from a broadcast made by Tangier Smith in 1937 to the effect that the latter had captured the only three giant pandas taken alive, of which one, Su-Lin, had been sold to members of another expedition. This implies that Ruth Harkness's account of Su-Lin's capture was a complete fabrication. It is difficult to credit this; but no purpose would be served by a re-discussion of this complex affair in what is primarily an attempt to collect up all known details of the habits of wild beishung. The ethics of some of the characters associated with the beishung trade in the 1930s left much to be desired. It can however be noted that in the summer of 1937 Tangier Smith is reported to have arrived in Shanghai with a fully grown female, which subsequently died during the voyage to Singapore, *en route* to London. On that expedition he had also obtained a large male, which died from blood-poisoning in a leg-wound – sustained during capture in the Wassu country – while on the journey down to the coast. And we can also note that while there are chronological gaps in Ruth Harkness's various accounts of her exploit, and their continuity is unsatisfactory, they do not read like fiction.

Nor is there anything fictional about the fact that in August 1937, only eight months after returning to America with Su-Lin, she was back again in Shanghai, determined to secure a mate for the supposedly female Su-Lin and financed on this second expedition by the $8,700 she had received for the latter from the Brookfield Zoo. By this time the Japanese had invaded China and, unable to enter Szechwan up the Yangtze, she was obliged to proceed by way of Hong Kong, Saigon and Hanoi, and thence by rail to Yunnan Fu and plane to Chengtu. This time she went in unaccompanied, since Quentin Young had gone off collecting in Indonesia. However, after she had camped for three months in the Wassu country once again, directing the operations of her native hunters, the latter actually secured her two cubs. One, which was half grown, died because it would eat nothing except bamboo. The other, not yet weaned, Ruth was able to carry back to Shanghai late in January 1938 and lodge in the Brookfield Zoo in February, where it was known first as Diana and subsequently as Mei-Mei.

That she was able to secure two cubs during this three-month expedition must be considered convincing proof that neither were beishung as scarce nor were their haunts as inaccessible as all previous reports by native hunters and Western explorers alike had indicated. That she, the most amateur of amateurs, might have been outrageously lucky on her first venture can be accepted, but equally lucky a second time – no! There must have been red faces at her achievement among the professional zoologists and other members of the generously endowed field-expeditions that had preceded her; and more red faces in December 1938 when Tangier Smith arrived in London with no fewer than five beishung, the survivors of *ten* he had collected.

As it happens, some details of this collection have been put on record for us by Rosa Loseby, who had a poor opinion of panda-collecting. On 24 December 1938 the *Field* published a letter from her as Hon. Secretary of the Dogs' Home in Kowloon, together with a unique photograph of Tangier's five beishung in the grounds of the home.

It sounds a formidable task [she wrote] to house five giant pandas, two blue sheep, a musk deer, a marmot, a golden-haired monkey, and three attendants in a well-filled dogs' home, built for about fifty dogs. But in fact it was not! Within two hours of the first inquiry, the collection and attendants had been unloaded, housed and settled down.

The condition of the animals after a three weeks' journey across China, skirting the war area, ending with two days on an overloaded tramp in heavy seas, had best be left to the imagination. But I would like to add an opinion that, if the zoos of the world must encourage this trade in wild animals, they should, at least, supervise the trade, and not leave it to private enterprise.

The giant pandas ranged in age from three years to ten months, and their weights from about 300 lb. to 50 lb. They seemed perfectly content in the open grass run, fastened with a leather collar and chained to an iron stake, but one rainy night I had to bring them into the kennels; after this, they were always restless out of doors, demanding permission to go inside, so much so that one pulled the stake out of the ground and marched straight up to the kennels, demanding admission.

The whole collection was absolutely fearless of human beings or even the dogs, with which the blue sheep rubbed noses through the wire within half an hour of arrival.

There cannot be the slightest doubt that, during the twelve days they were with me, the animals all made remarkable improvement in condition. They were just beginning to show their joy of life and assert their independence when they were recrated for the journey to the zoo.

It is only fair to add that the animals showed that their owner, Mr Smith, had a remarkable knowledge of animals and their needs, but this does not alter the fact that a wealthy public body, like the Zoo, could afford to spend much more on their animals than a private trader, and should do so, or not encourage the trade.

This consignment of Hsi-fan animals had in fact been intended for the USA; but Smith's asking-price was too high for the Bronx Zoo, so Ming (a seven-month-old female) and two adult males, Tang and Sung, were purchased by the London Zoological Society, while Happy (a three- or four-year-old female) was sold to a German dealer and exhibited at various German zoos before ultimately being acquired by the St Louis Zoo. Ming survived until 1944, but Tang and Sung died after a few months in captivity.

From the naturalist's point of view it can, again, only be described as tragic that Ruth Harkness apparently left no account of this second expedition, nor of a third which she undertook in April 1938 in yet another attempt to secure a male cub, as mate in this instance for Mei-Mei, for whom she had received $8,500. But her success, and that of Tangier Smith also, in 'bringing 'em back alive' had opened up new possibilities. Henceforward the demand would be not for dead beishung for show-cases and panoramic groups but for live ones for exhibition in zoological gardens.

Since Tangier Smith's price was too high the Bronx Zoo sought elsewhere for beishung, and in April 1938 Dean Sage implored Professor Dickinson of the West China University at Chengtu to obtain live cubs for this zoo. In response to this desperate appeal the professor contacted a former missionary-cum-hunter, Den Wei-han, who was able to buy a cub, four or five months old, from a native of O Lung Kuan, 'the Village of the Sleeping Dragon', some sixty miles from Chengtu. After being taught to feed by Dr Graham, this cub, Pandora, reached New York on 10 June.

In the meantime the Chinese Foreign Office, alarmed by the wholesale export during the previous years of their unique 'bear', announced in April 1939 that further expeditions by Western collectors to secure beishung would not be encouraged. Nevertheless, Wei-han had already obtained a second cub, Pan, for the Bronx Zoo; while in the autumn of that year an American newspaperman acquired another cub, which had been captured when two months old in a locality 150 miles from Chengtu. This was Mei-Lan, who in November began his long captivity in the Brookfield Zoo.

Then in the early summer of 1941 Dr Graham was informed that the Chinese Goverment wished to secure a live beishung, which Mme Chiang Kai-shek would present to the American people in appreciation of gifts to the Chinese people received through the United China Relief organization. Graham contacted the reliable Wei-han, and two groups of hunters were engaged in the Weichow and Tsao-Po country around Wenchuan. During July and August Graham himself made a five-week expedition to this region, to find that his hunters had been able to secure only one beishung, and that this had escaped.

Summer was a difficult season to hunt beishung, when the trees were in leaf and the undergrowth heavy, and when, in addition, the local hunters, all farmers, were reluctant to leave their crops, in order to act as guides; whereas in the clearer weather of late autumn, when the leaves had fallen, tracking the beishung over fresh snow was more practicable, while the farmers were then glad to supplement their income by acting as beaters with their dogs through the bamboo-thickets.

However, since the Bronx directors insisted that they must have a beishung by October, Graham returned to Wenchuan in September to organize a force of seventy Wassu hunters with forty dogs, allotted to seven different localities. This, the largest-scale beishung hunt on record at that time, resulted only in the purchase of a single cub about six months old from a local official sixty miles distant; but a few days after Graham had left Tsao-Po his hunters did succeed in securing another cub near Lung Kuan. Although this one was a ten- or eleven-month-old male, weighing some sixty pounds, they were able to capture it with their hands and transport it to Chengtu by 24 October, some three weeks after the other cub. These two, Pan-Dah and Pan-Dee, stayed at Graham's house at the University until the middle of November, when John Tee-Van arrived from New York to accompany them to America.

Mme Chiang's address at the presentation ceremony of Pan-Dah and Pan-Dee can be cited as a permanent, tragic memorial to the perpetual ironic futility of the affairs of nations. It was 4 a.m. when she spoke to America from the newly opened radio-station at Chungking, still scarred from Japanese bombing attacks.

Through the United China Relief, you, our American friends, are alleviating the sufferings of our people and are binding the wounds which have been wantonly inflicted upon them through no fault of their own. As a very small way of saying 'Thank you', we would like to present to America, through you, Mr Tee-Van, this pair of comical, black and white, furry pandas. We hope that their cute antics will bring as much joy to the American children as American friendship has brought to our Chinese people.

Five years later China's gratitude to the Western world was again in evidence, when in the late autumn of 1945 the Szechwan authorities organized an even larger search, involving two hundred Wassu, for a beishung which the Chinese Government could present to Britain as a replacement for Ming, who had died after six years at Regent's Park; and after two months' hunting the Wassu captured a twelve-month-old female, to be named Lien-Ho or Unity.

Lien-Ho, who died of pneumonia in 1950, was the last beishung to reach the West until 1958 saw the arrival of the most widely known of all: Chi-Chi. When captured in Szechwan in December 1957 by agents of the Peking Zoo she was about six months old and the youngest of three cubs taken at that time. As it happened, an American zoo had previously commissioned an Austrian animal-collector, Heini Demmer, who was then living in Nairobi, to negotiate the exchange of a large consignment of East African animals for one giant panda. In due course Demmer set out for Peking and in May 1958 selected Chi-Chi as the most suitable of the three. In the meantime, however, the USA had placed an embargo on all goods imported from the now 'Red' China. So, that summer, the unfortunate Chi-Chi toured various European zoos, including Copenhagen, Frankfurt and Berlin-Friederichs-felde, and ultimately visited London early in September for an intended stay of three weeks. However, at the end of that month she was bought by the Zoological Society with financial aid from Granada TV, and immediately proved one of the zoo's most popular exhibits.

In the meantime a two- or three-year-old male, Ping-Ping, had been transferred from Peking to Moscow in 1957; and he was followed two years later by An-An. These were to be the last beishung to go west. In twenty-three years seventeen had been exhibited outside China, and not less than sixty more had been purchased as skins, shot by collectors for museums, or had died in transit from Hsi-fan to the outside world, since Weigold had obtained the first beishung skin of this century in 1914; but

The young Chi-Chi with Heini Demmer at Frankfurt. (*Tierbilder Okapia*)

The young An-An, the last beishung to come to Europe. *(Tierbilder Okapia)*

The Peking trio of cubs in 1956. *(Eastfoto, New York)*

henceforward giant pandas were to be an exclusively Communist possession.

The Peking Zoo had been reopened in 1950, after being a private zoological garden of the Empress Dowager Tse Hsi during the early years of the century. In the summer of 1955 the zoo had acquired three beishung cubs; and these were followed by an adult male and female the following year and another female, Li-Li, in 1957. By 1963 there were seven beishung in various Chinese zoos. On 9 September that year Peking's Li-Li gave birth to Ming-Ming, and on 4 September the following year to twins, of which only one, Lin-Lin, survived. By 1965 Peking's six-year-old Pi-Pi and Li-Li and their cub and yearling had been joined by another pair less than twelve months old and by an immature female; and there were four more males and a young male in other Chinese zoos. By 1966 this total of twelve had been increased to eighteen or more, including a pair in North Korea's Pyongyang zoo. When Caroline Jarvis, editor of the *International Zoo Year-Book,* visited China for three weeks in September 1965 she found that Chinese zoologists were undertaking serious research into 'the natural history, conservation, and classification of their very varied and, in many instances, unique fauna'. During the previous fifteen years more zoos had been opened up in China than in any other country in the world, while the Chinese people were being made aware of their wildlife heritage by 'beautiful stamp issues depicting giant pandas, golden-haired monkeys, Manchurian cranes, butterflies and fishes', and by pictures of these portrayed on handbags, scarves, tobacco-tins, cups, glasses and many other household objects.

Although the zoologist's world knows few international boundaries it may be some time before we in the West obtain further information about China's beishung, wild or captive; and I have not personally been able to make any contact with Chinese zoologists since the Year of the Red Guards. However, those wild beishung in the rugged bamboo jungles of Hsi-fan should be safe from any disturbance.

CHAPTER FIVE

Reactions to Men and Dogs

Those who collected wild beishung left pitifully threadbare accounts of their habits; but such observers as there have been, whether Western or native, are all agreed that they are extremely conservative in their choice of habitat, seldom entering the higher rhododendron belt above the bamboo jungle and avoiding the hot canyons below. The Roosevelts were perhaps correct in suggesting that their geographical range is not continuous but distributed in pockets in separate zones of those broad bands of bamboo that flank the steep sides of every valley at altitudes of between 5,000 and 13,000 feet; though according to Ivor Montagu they are concentrated throughout their habitat mainly in the zone around 10,000 or 10,500 feet, rarely descending below 8,500 feet or ascending higher than 11,500.

Within the narrow limits of our knowledge of their life-history, there does not appear to be any pressing reason why beishung should ever venture out of the jungle, since they are surrounded by their inexhaustible supply of bamboo food. Moreover, although some are, as we have seen, taken accidentally in spear-traps and pitfalls or shot in trees, and a few young ones are picked out of hollow trees by hunters and woodcutters – to die quickly in captivity from lack of proper food – they have suffered less disturbance through the centuries than almost any other mammal, for they were apparently rarely hunted for their meat or skins by native inhabitants of Hsi-fan until Western explorers began offering cash for them dead or alive. The skins of other animals, and especially the 'golden fleece' of the takin, are much more attractive to the local hunters, since those of the beishung are too coarse to make comfortable garments; nor are the natives interested in black and white rugs, nor apparently in comfortable sleeping-mats, despite the fact that the beishung's thick, woolly fur is wiry and forms a dense, springy surface. And although Ralf von Koenigswald, investigator of *Pithecanthropus,* is reported to have discovered many teeth and bones of a large extinct form of beishung in Chinese apothecaries' shops, *Ailuropoda melanoeuca*'s organs do not seem, curiously enough, to have been prized as ingredients for China's almost universal medical quackery. The natives themselves had no incentive to hunt and kill an animal that never attacked them or their stock and very rarely damaged their maize crops. Was not the beishung *Ho-shien,* the harmless 'monk' among bears? Indeed, his only misdemeanour was sometimes to raid their beehives, fashioned from hollow tree-trunks, although these were protected by strong fences. But the Lo-Los made no attempt to kill these raiders, though they might wound one in the course of driving it away. To these aboriginals the beishung was supernatural and divine, and the Roosevelts observed that although great celebrations were held on the night that they shot their beishung these were qualified by superstitious and religious scruples. Initially, indeed, they were not allowed to

48

take the beishung's body into the village compound; and when they were eventually permitted to put it in an out-of-the-way hayloft, they were informed that after their departure a priest would be summoned to conduct a purification ceremony.

Their liking for honey is one reason why the beishung should venture outside the bamboo and come into contact with man, and but for this craving they would be even less known. A curious feature of the beishung's anatomy is that his oesophagus is furnished with a tough, horny lining, and his thick-walled stomach is so muscular that it resembles a gizzard. These organs are therefore well protected against fragments of sharp bamboo, which could prove formidable objects for any digestive tract to cope with, even after being crushed by the beishung's huge molars. Yet, by contrast, his intestines are quite unprotected and instead of being extra-long, as in the case of other herbivorous mammals, are short even for a carnivore, to which order the beishung is assigned by reason of his bone-structure and teeth. It has therefore been suggested that the oesophagus's horny lining serves in fact as a protection against the stings of bees when the beishung is raiding hives.

It may be that the beishung venture down into the inhabited valley bottoms more often than has been appreciated by Westerners. Schäfer observed that they often made use on their nocturnal expeditions of man-made paths. 'Once I found traces only five metres from an inhabited woodcutter's hut, to which the panda had apparently come by accident. Another time I found traces in a deserted hut, right by the fireplace.' Sheldon tracked one that had climbed a small pine tree on an open slope above the village of Tsapei, within two hundred yards and in full sight of a farmhouse, though the nearest bamboo was on the other side of the valley beyond the Chengou. This beishung had allowed the farmer to approach to within sixty feet of its tree when, on the latter firing his old matchlock, it climbed down.

The beishung's arboreal activities would appear to have been underestimated. They take refuge in trees from the hunters' hounds, and no doubt from wild dogs too; and the favourite resting-places of captive beishung during the day are tree-like structures, in the crotches of which they half-sit, half-recline, with sharply arched backs. Chi-Chi gave an exhibition of her

49

Ming-Ming indulging the cub's taste for tree-climbing . . . *(Eastfoto)*

. . . and a hesitant Chi-Chi, old enough to know better. *(C. Guggisberg, Nairobi)*

climbing ability shortly after arriving at Regent's Park, mounting the steps to her enclosure and clambering over the gate at the top of them before lumbering off excitedly through the crowds. According to Sheldon, wild beishung can climb conifers of all kinds – in order to sun themselves, say the natives; and Weigold saw one sitting in the crown of a birch tree in the middle of a steep bamboo jungle. Although captive beishung have been described as astonishingly clumsy climbers, and no doubt increasing weight may hamper them as they mature, the young climb persistently and almost as nimbly as cats, according to Ruth Harkness. On vertical or near-vertical trees their technique is similar to that of bears. Embracing the trunk, with the soles of all four feet pressed against the bark, they swarm up with a series of looping 'caterpillar' movements, taking advantage of branches and snags to hoist themselves. They lower themselves down tail first, unless the tree is inclined at an angle gentle enough for them to walk down head first, relying more on the friction of their soles against the bark than on the 'bite' of their claws, though they will check themselves with the latter if they slip. Karl Schneider, who studied Happy during the latter's residence in Leipzig Zoo, noted how carefully he would place his hind feet when climbing down from his tree, and how, if the drop was too steep, he would turn through a hundred and eighty degrees and, shifting his balance, let himself down bottom first; but if in doubt as to how to get down, he would position himself close to the trunk and crawl down.

Schäfer stated that wild beishung were shy and timid, shunning open places in the forest. But they have no reason to be, and the experience of other Westerners, and natives for that matter, does not appear to support this contention. On the contrary, what other large mammal would allow men to approach so closely and so noisily through the jungle? And a beishung has good ears, nose and eyes. Sheldon, in a mistaken allusion to the beishung's stupidity, describes how: 'On one occasion at a distance of 350 yards I observed two individuals on the edge of a bamboo jungle. Driven out by four dogs and warned by several high-powered bullets whistling about their ears, neither animal even broke into a run' – as if these particular beishung had ever had high-powered bullets whistling about them previously! And again: 'Dean Sage and I observed another panda pursued by four dogs. In this instance he *walked* to within eight feet of Dean and was stopped only by bullets. He gave absolutely no evidence that he saw either of us, and seemed completely to disregard both the shots and the loud talking and shouts of a few minutes previous.'

Obviously there can be no such thing as a *stupid* wild mammal, because such an animal would very quickly be eliminated by predators, though possibly one in several thousand manages to survive adolescence despite a degree of mental derangement, as seems to have been the case in one or two instances among tigers. But, in general, a stupid mammal is a contradiction in terms. A wild beishung cannot be expected to appreciate, without previous experience, that high-powered bullets are dangerous and that one must run away from them. In the wild state certain areas of a beishung's brain are not normally employed; but when he is confronted with new situations in captivity he has the intelligence to cope with them. The Director of the Brookfield Zoo considered Su-Lin to be highly intelligent and able to tackle problems beyond the capabilities of any of the monkeys then in the zoo. Unable to reach a shelf with food on it, for example, he pushed a wicker basket near the shelf, and by climbing on it achieved his objective. Schneider noted the practical and skilful way in which the three- or four-year-old Happy handled his food-tin in order to lick out every part of it, or edged his water-bowl about a short distance at a time, as young brown bears would also do. Young beishung evidently learn early, for Ming-Ming, the first cub to be born in captivity, 'shrieked at anything that seemed threatening and was responsive to sound' when only a few months old. 'If we called out his name two metres away, he never failed to turn back and come to us.' And Ruth Harkness relates how, on revisiting Su-Lin at the Brookfield Zoo after an absence of two months, she found 'her' '. . . lying lazily on her back in the play-pen, toying with a few leaves of spinach, occasionally taking a nibble at one of them.

' "Su-Lin!" I called.

'Slowly she got up and looked at me. I drew nearer and she started to climb over the edge of the pen; when I touched her she made a lunge for me and landed in my arms.'

So too the young Chi-Chi would react immediately to her foster-father's voice when she could not see him but only hear him through a half-open door, and had no difficulty in recognizing her Frankfurt keeper among a group of several people. Subsequently, when as a seven-year-old adult she had savaged her keeper so severely that he was off work for seven months, she recognized him instantly on his return, growling and pacing up and down her enclosure angrily.

53

But if beishung are not afraid of men, they certainly are of dogs. When hunting a beishung, the Wassu would set their dogs on a fresh trail and follow it up as swiftly as possible, without halting, until the animal was overtaken and a shot obtained; and Schäfer observed that after being hunted by dogs the beishung would disappear from their accustomed haunts for a few days, or longer. Their fear of dogs is evidently inherent, for when Chi-Chi was on exhibition at Frankfurt she was very sensitive to their barking, while Su-Lin was so terrified of the barking of the dingoes in the next cage at the Brookfield Zoo that he had to be moved to another compartment, and so terrified subsequently of the smell of dogs at a farm in the country that he refused his food and moaned all night, forcing Ruth Harkness to return with him to the noisy sanctuary of her New York flat! And these were the reactions of a cub only two months old that had been removed from its wild environment a couple of weeks after birth.

One feels that such violent inbred reactions must be due to terror of that scourge which even tigers fear and are prey to, the hunting pack of wild dogs, rather than to fear of the domestic hounds of hunters with which comparatively few beishung will ever have come in contact. But although Sheldon stated that wild dogs – red wolves, as they are known in Hsi-fan – were often to be heard hunting in packs at night in the beishung's country, and that young beishung might be killed by them, virtually nothing appears to be known of the habits of these fiery-red Asian wild dogs, except that they are definitely present in western Hsi-fan. According to Wilson, they quickly kill or drive out all other game. When after pheasants, one afternoon in 1908, he saw a pack of eight or ten of them within a mile of the hamlet of Tatchienchi at the foot of Wa Shan. 'There were three or four together and very brazen, allowing me to approach within 100 yards of them before they moved slowly off. Wild pigs are common in this neighbourhood, and on one occasion Mr Zappey saw a pig attacked and partly devoured in a few minutes by three of these wild dogs.'

When cornered by hunters' dogs – which do not normally display that fear of a beishung that they do of black bears – a beishung does not apparently make an attempt to escape, but may grab a dog with his forefeet, pull it to him and inflict terrible

54

wounds with his powerful jaws. His teeth, rather than his strong forearms with their very sharp, hooked claws, appear to be his main line of defence; though it must be noted that Happy, who would usually adopt a menacing attitude when confronted by strangers, would stretch out his arms in front of him, draw in his head and threaten to strike with his paws. But, knowing the proven ability of a pack of wild dogs to tear a tiger to pieces, there is little doubt that they could do the same to an adult beishung, though they would have more difficulty in getting to grips with the latter's massively compact body and in penetrating his dense mat of fur.

CHAPTER SIX

Enemies and Neighbours

What other predators are there in the bamboo jungles that might disturb or drive out the beishung? There is no evidence as to whether lynx ever enter the bamboo. A lynx would in any case be no match for an adult beishung, though it could kill a cub. Black bears, which are very numerous in the rhododendron zone and beech forests in the winter, and in the cornfields in the summer, certainly enter the bamboo. So too do the blue bears, which, though usually regarded as inhabitants of the steppes, normally winter in the mountains (or do so in northern Sikang)

where abundant food is available, especially in the forests of prickly oak, at that season when the steppe vegetation is buried under snow – for not all bears hibernate. Both these bears might occasionally kill a beishung cub, and must sometimes come face to face with an adult on the game-trails that are driven like tunnels through the dense thickets of bamboo, from five to fifteen feet in height, overlaid by snow.

Although these tunnels are usually referred to as the beishung's special trails, they are commonly used by other large mammals, such as leopards and wild pigs, the latter of which are very numerous up to a height of eight thousand feet. Since they are, by all accounts, too large to have been opened up by the solitary-living beishung, one suspects that they were first engineered by the powerful takin, which, standing more than four feet at the shoulder, are as big as small bullocks and much more heavily built. The bamboo jungle is almost as much a sanctuary for the takin as it is for the beishung. Not only do they retreat into the bamboo when disturbed, but they also pass most of the winter days in the bamboo and rhododendron thickets, browsing the bamboo leaves and tramping down those broad, well-defined trails to all points of the compass, in their passage to and from the salt-licks. So commonly indeed are takin and beishung to be found inhabiting the same jungles that the presence of the former in a certain district has been cited as proof that it is also inhabited by beishung, even though no beishung have ever been reported from that area.

The inhabitants of Hsi-fan, both Chinese and native, are much afraid of Yeh-niu, the wild cow, and the Wassu told Fergusson that if a member of a herd was wounded the remainder would charge over the hunter. But rather than cattle the takin more closely resemble gigantic Rocky Mountain goats, both in their heavy build and in their short but immensely thick legs and feet. A humped back, a roman nose, curved, black, gnu-like horns, short, 'cut-off' ears and short, goat-like tail all contribute to the takin's unique appearance. But despite his apparently clumsy lumbering gait he is as agile as a chamois over the rough ground he inhabits and can scale almost vertical cliffs. Fergusson described the takin's country around Wenchuan (and this was also of course beishung country):

Takin. *(Zoological Society of London)*

In some places the path would lead us along a narrow ridge where a slip of a foot on either side would land us at the foot of a precipice several hundred feet below. Again, we would climb staircases made by notching a log and setting it on end against the cliffs; in other places sticks of wood were tied to uprights by creepers, and up these we had to climb until it made our heads giddy to look down. How the takin makes his way about in such country is a mystery to me, but in the early spring here he is to be found, during his short migration from the sheltered valley in which he has passed the winter to the grassy plains where he feeds during the summer months.

Père David, of course, was aware of the presence of this extraordinary animal in Hsi-fan, but no factual evidence of its existence reached the Western world until 1850, when B. H. Hodgson acquired three skins while exploring Tibet; and it was 1907 before one was shot, to the north of Tatsienlu, by the American consul at Chungking. It is now recognized that there are three races of takin, which has been classed with the musk-ox for want of a more plausible relationship – one race inhabiting Bhutan and Assam; a second Szechwan; and the third the Tsingling Shan mountains. It is the bulls of this third race which are conspicuously golden in the sunlight. 'Huge golden-yellow brutes, moving easily amid the bamboo jungle on a slope so steep that they seemed to be hanging by their horns,' wrote the American explorer and naturalist R. C. Andrews, when hunting them in these mountains in the autumn of 1921:

Everything about them seemed unreal – the great Roman nose, the cow-like horns and the clumsy body, glistening in the sun like molten gold against a background of dull green leaves. The takin of the 'golden fleece' is really golden in colour. From the end of their enormous noses to the tips of their abbreviated tails, these Shensi animals are a golden-yellow without a patch of darker shading.

We watched them for half an hour, hoping that they would settle themselves for their midday rest. But they continued to browse upon the bamboo leaves, always moving slowly upwards to the timber line at 11,000 feet, and an alpine meadow of thick long brown grass at the edge of the rhododendrons.

But, other than wild dogs, the only predator that could be a serious threat to the young beishung is the leopard, though an adult would probably prove too powerful an adversary. Here again it is possibly significant that Su-Lin, on first arriving in New York, showed signs of unease when held up to the Chinese Ambassador's daughter, who was wearing a leopardskin waist-coat. But although Sage and Sheldon saw the fresh track of a leopard crossing their path when they were almost twelve thousand feet up in the Chen Liang Shan, Wilson stated that leopards were scarce in western Szechwan, though common southwards of Omei Shan into Yunnan; and apparently no more is known about leopards in Hsi-fan than about wild dogs. We know less indeed about the habits of all these Hsi-fan mammals than about any other community of large mammals in the world, even those of Amazonia, and it is impossible to determine whether the beishung's life-history is influenced in any way by any of them.

Père David, it will be recalled, made passing reference to tigers in the forests above Muping; but long before his day Marco Polo had reported that 'striped lions' inhabited Szechwan and Yunnan, and that Kublai Khan hunted with them:

They are bigger than Babylonian lions, and their skins are coloured in the most beautiful way, being striped all along the sides with black, red and white. They are very skilful in catching boars, wild cattle and asses, bears, deer, gazelles and other game. It is a magnificent sight when the lion is released and pursues its prey with fierce appetite, until it has caught up with it through its great speed. For such purposes His Majesty takes these hunting-lions with him in cages that stand on carts; each lion is accompanied by a dog, with which it soon makes friends. The lions have to be shut in these cages, because otherwise, as soon as they caught sight of game, they would be unable to restrain themselves and would savagely pursue it. Also they must be brought close to the prey against the wind, so that the animals shall not scent them too soon and escape.

However, no contemporary Westerner seems to have encountered a tiger in Hsi-fan; nor are there any reports of tigers preying on beishung. But they are, or were, certainly present in beishung country, for one was killed over bait on the upper Min, at midwinter a few years before Weigold's expedition. R. L. Jack heard many tales about tigers when he was at Ka-La Ba, some seventy-five miles west of Yehli, in 1900; and both Wilson and A. E. Pratt reported them from the Wa Shan jungles, fifty miles to the north-east. Pratt, who was some ten years earlier in the field than Wilson, referred to them as being very numerous, in contrast to Wilson, who stated that they were uncommon except in the Chiench'ang valley of the Yangtze on the Szechwan–Yunnan border. It was more than four thousand feet up on the snow-covered hills above this valley that H. R. Davies described how, in February 1900:

> Soon after starting the next morning we heard the roaring of a tiger in the hills to the west across the river. Finally he came out and lay down on a big rock to sun himself. He was about 600 yards off on a steep hillside. The tiger did not seem in the least disturbed by our watching him, nor by the presence of several people who were going along a path on his side of the river about 500 foot below him. I took my field-glasses and watched him for quite five minutes: he would sometimes get up and walk around for a few yards and then lie down again on the rock, flapping the end of his tail. Eventually he got up and walked away into the jungle. This is the first tiger I have seen or heard of in western China.

Wilson was also told that pilgrims were sometimes killed by tigers on the sacred mountain of Omei (north-west of Wa Shan), near the summit of which there was an image of one; and R. F. Johnston refers in 1906 to a legend associated with the Black Water stream near the mountain's ancient monastery of Wa-nien. This was to the effect that when, in the days of the T'ang dynasty, a wandering monk arrived at the stream and was searching for a ford, in order to cross over and set up a hermitage on the far bank, a large tiger appeared out of the middle of the torrent and carried him across on its back. Today Tiger Bridge still stands witness to this miracle.

Traditions of tigers were evidently strong throughout Hsi-fan. Graham's Wassu hunters, for instance, relied for success on the mountain god Wu T'sang, which was represented by a stone image standing on its hands on the back of a tiger; though if their objective was to capture a beishung alive another deity, Mei Shan, in the form of a flat stone, was invoked. The hunters did not, however, appear to have much faith in these and other deities, for although they made offerings to them, or promises of gifts of wine, chicken and pigs, and burnt candles and incense before their images, they were liable, if unsuccessful in their hunting, to whip them or throw them to the ground.

Meagre though these notes on possible predators are, it is clear that *Ailuropoda melanoleuca* can never have been seriously threatened by any of them, and every aspect of his tranquil habits and slow-moving gait confirms that his kind have enjoyed a leisured, trouble-free existence for a very long time. 'During the course of tracking different animals for several miles,' wrote Sheldon, 'I never saw a sign of one travelling faster than a walk.' His swiftest gait is indeed a clumsy, pigeon-toed trot with lifted forepaw curved inward. Although a beishung can, like a bear, assume an erect posture, he walks only on all fours, with a more rolling and waddling gait than a bear and a considerably longer stride, while his heavy head sways from side to side well below the line of his shoulder. Since a beishung lacks the hind heel-pad of a bear, retaining only the plantar pad, which is covered with hair, he walks on a cushion of hair with only the sole of his forefoot full upon the ground. This thick mat of hair may possibly protect his feet from splintered stumps of dead bamboo culms; but it is probably of greater service to him in obtaining a purchase on the steep ice- and snow-covered slopes, up which he climbs with unexpected agility.

An animal of such reputedly solitary habits, and so relatively few in numbers, could hardly have survived for so many millennia had it been extensively preyed upon. What purpose, then, is served by the beishung's dramatic parti-colouring? – assuming, that is, that there must always be cause and effect in Nature's scheme. His colour-pattern is unique among the carnivora. Bold black and white in a shaded habitat, in which visibility is measured in yards or feet and a beishung is invisible, to the human eye at least, at a distance of thirty yards! Skunk and ratel (the honey-badger) display this same pattern, associated in their case with the possession of the animal world's most powerful stink-glands. A beishung too has a very large glandular area normally covered by his short broad tail; but this does not apparently give off any odour perceptible to the human nose, though the lesser panda does emit a musky odour from its smaller glandular area when it is excited. The beishung's colour-pattern therefore advertises the fact that his powerful jaws make him a dangerous adversary to any prospective predator – but what predator? His colour-pattern is obliterative and cryptically concealing in the aisles of bamboos, and among the rocks and snow outside the jungle (though extremely conspicuous on snow-free ground and in trees, as Edgar may have observed) – but a camouflage against what predator? Schneider's statement that bears with white markings invariably rise on their hind legs when attacked, but the beishung does not, would appear to be irrelevant; and one must agree with Davis Dwight, who undertook a monumental morphological study of the beishung, that its dramatic colouring is not a bio-logical pattern conditioned by natural selection, and has no more significance than a black Galloway stirk's white belt.

We have considered possible predators whom the beishung may encounter in and out of the bamboo jungle. What other neighbours has he? Descending the altitudinal scale, there are the blue sheep on the alpine grasslands and steppes. Below them in the densest upper forest of spruce, silver fir and larch where the undergrowth is thin, and also out on the open screes, at altitudes of from eight to fourteen thousand feet, are the little musk deer, standing only three feet high at the shoulder. By day they hide up in the forest, often resting on the upper half of a sloping deadfall, lying close to the trunk, and venturing out in the early morning and at dusk to dig and scrape for herbage among the rocks or under the snow with their slender, ivory-white, dagger-like tusks. Only the inaccessibility of their habitat can have preserved the musk deer from extermination. For centuries the males have been relentlessly persecuted by Chinese trappers for the skin gland or pod, the size of a small hen's egg, which develops in the male's genitals during the rutting season. In Wilson's day 60,000 pods were being brought into Tatsienlu annually, and Jack Young noted that the annual export from Tatsienlu alone amounted to the value of £20,000. Every Paris perfumery had agents buying up musk-pods in the remote mountain villages of the Tibetan borders; and west Szechwan is still the major musk-producer in China, though some deer are now 'farmed' for their pods at Markang, in the north-west of the province.

Below the musk deer are the timid tufted deer, which rarely venture out of their mixed woods of primeval conifers (with dwarf rhododendron underbrush), willow, birch and prickly oak. On the wild, precipitous ridges of these forests, too, lives the commonest large mammal in Hsi-fan – the white-maned serow of the melancholy, elongated face and exceedingly long ears. *Ai-Han-tsze*, the cliff donkey, hides up in the forest by day and grazes on the grassy slopes early in the morning and late in the evening; as does that extraordinary goat-antelope the goral, though the latter is seldom to be found actually within the forest.

These neighbours the beishung may sometimes encounter when he wanders out of the jungle; but with him in the bamboo are the little panda, the takin and the muntjac, who, like the European roe deer, may venture as far abroad as the village corn-fields. No doubt, too, the troops of a hundred or more golden snub-nosed monkeys pass through the bamboo from time to time, while swinging through the high remote conifer and beech forests of Kansu, Szechwan and the Tsinling mountains, where the snow lies for half the year.

If we know a very little, and can infer rather more, about the life of the beishung in the wild state, that of the golden monkey is a closed book, for it approaches human settlements even less often than the beishung, though the Roosevelts shot nine out of a troop near Lunchingsa. Its existence has, however, long been known to the Chinese and it is portrayed by them on vases and silk-paintings as a kind of grinning dragon with a turquoise-blue face and tail and a fiery red breast. But to the West this 'dragon' was only another of the Chinese stylistic conventions, and Chinese literary allusions certainly did nothing to dispel this belief. Thus while one author, Hai-tul, noted correctly that its nose turned upwards, he added that: 'Its tail is very long and forked at the end; whenever it rains, the animal thrusts the fork

Muntjac. *(Zoological Society of London)*

into its nose. It goes in herds and lives in friendship; when one dies the rest accompany it to burial. Its activity is so great that it runs its head against the trees.'

It was left to Père David to dispel another myth, and in his diary for 4 May at Muping he was able to announce that: 'My hunters, who left a fortnight ago for the eastern regions, return today and bring me six monkeys of a new species which the Chinese call *chiu-tsiu-hou,* or golden-brown monkey. The animals are very robust and have large, muscular limbs. Their faces are very strange, green-blue or turquoise with the nose turned up almost to the forehead. Their tails are long and strong. Their backs are covered with long hair and they live in trees in the highest mountains, now white with snow.'

Milne-Edwards could make nothing of this large, bizarre langur almost five feet in length (including its twenty-eight-inch tail), with its bright blue face, red cheeks and brow and dark brown eyes, and was constrained to name it *Rhinopithecus roxellanae*, after Roxellana, the beautiful slave with the retroussé nose who became the wife of Suleiman the Magnificent. To this natural and unnatural history we can, it seems, add little, though breeding troops have recently been established successfully in three Chinese zoos.

CHAPTER SEVEN

From Bamboo Jungle
to Tibetan Steppe

It will be recalled that back in the 1880s the Russian explorer Berezovski had reported beishung in the Tsinling range of mountains between Szechwan and Kansu, far to the north of the accepted limits of their range. However, this record had long been forgotten, in the belief that beishung were strictly confined to the bamboo jungles, when in 1938 Sheldon found their droppings high up on the Liang Shan mountains, a thousand feet above the rhododendron belt and probably fifteen hundred feet above the nearest bamboo. From this incident he deduced that they must sometimes venture out of the bamboo to explore the treeless grasslands of the blue-sheep country. But though he believed that they were to some degree nomadic, he could never have supposed that some individual beishung may visit the blue-sheep steppes regularly. However two years later, on the morning of 10 June 1940, a young Chinese zoologist, Hung-shou Pen, a member of a Natural Resources Exploration expedition, arrived at the upper source of the Yellow River, at that point where it connects the two lakes Tsaring Nor and Oring Nor on the steppe between the immense ranges of the Bayan Kara Shan and the Amne Machen Shan, which the American explorer Leonard Clark believed to be higher than any ranges in the Himalayas. With a youthful enthusiasm recalling to this armchair explorer his own red-letter days with the red deer on those lesser steppes of the Cairngorm mosses, Pen describes what awaited him in this unknown land of Koko Nor, or Tsinghai Province.

After jumping over some rills we came to a boggy tract. Suddenly our guide and bodyguard uttered a loud cry of surprise. About 2-3,000 metres south-east of our route there emerged a queer beast. Hurriedly I took up my telescope and got a clear view of the beast with two cubs. 'Giant Panda! Giant Panda! Look, quick! How beautiful she is!' I could not help but cry out. At that moment we were on this side of one branch of the Yellow River. We were obliged to ford the river on horseback. In the meantime I was fortunate in obtaining many views of this rare animal. The mother with her cubs was just turning away from us, doubtless on account of the noise we made. In the course of their retreat the mother panda sauntered forth leisurely and stubbed plants for breakfast. Her fur is sparklingly bright as the sun shines upon it. Further away near the lake, the Oring Nor, many antelopes and wild asses were to be seen, all enjoying themselves happily. Two blue bears appeared on the opposite bank of the stream, where we were to ford across. None of these animals can compare in beauty with the giant panda. The colour of the two cubs is paler than that of the mother animal. They followed and suckled their mother [sic] as does a little pig or calf. Later they turned back and suddenly flashed before us in all their beauty. Our guide and bodyguard drove them away by shouting. They were then frightened and hurried away.

Oring Nor lies at 34° 7′ north, 97° 45′ east. These beishung watched by Pen were therefore not only a little farther north than those reported by Berezovski, but upwards of three hundred miles farther west than any previously recorded, with the exception of Edgar's unconfirmed sighting of one in a tree near Batang, three hundred and fifty miles to the south-east. We do not know whether those beishung inhabiting bamboo jungles bordering on the steppes are regular summer visitors to these. Pen's guide informed him that they were not, unlike the blue bears that followed their camps and were constantly to be seen digging out pikas (mouse-hares) and other small rodents. On the other hand the guide's further statement that beishung skins were rarely seen in the market at Sining, the capital of Tsinghai Province, and did not fetch such a good price as those of the blue bear because of the coarse texture of their fur, indicates that they do occur on the steppes with some regularity – a probability confirmed by the news of fresh sightings in 1966 in the hills to the north of Sining, some two hundred and fifty miles north-east of Oring Nor. Pen's discovery of them on the open steppes disposes of Brocklehurst's doubt as to their presence there because of the absence of bamboos.

Commenting on their presence on the steppes, Pen goes on to point out that, because the Tibetan plateau lies adjacent to the high mountain ranges of western Szechwan and of the north-Sikang–east-Tibet marches, the steppe animals have comparatively easy access to the mountain country. Bears in particular are always prepared to migrate long distances, and indeed where the zone of bamboo jungle is restricted they are sometimes found in the same jungles as beishung. If, Pen continues, the beishung do in fact inhabit those high mountains of western and central Szechwan that border on the Tibetan highlands, then there is nothing to prevent them migrating westwards, even as far north as the steppe sources of the lakes. A summer migration to that region would lead them through the fertile valley of the Ma Chu, as the upper Hwang Ho is known, and up onto the steppe where vegetation is also abundant, as are pikas and fish which, according

An-An relaxing. *(Zoological Society of London)*

to Pen's guide, both bears and beishung eat; whereas at this season the accumulation of snow in the bamboo jungles is still unmelted, and the fresh shoots of the bamboo have grown into unpalatable thickets.

Pen's argument is of course oversimplified, and draws some erroneous conclusions. *The* outstanding feature of the beishung's life-history, as we have seen, is the fact that he lives literally surrounded by food in the form of an inexhaustible supply of bamboo. That is the primary reason why he so seldom leaves the jungle. Normally he has no need to migrate, unlike bears, which, after denning up in December, often have to travel many miles in search of food when they emerge from hibernation in May or June.

Nor was Pen correct in his assumption that the bamboo-shoots would be unpalatable in the summer. On the contrary, young shoots continue springing up from June until the end of September, according to altitude and species, and the wild beishung is not particular as to what kind of bamboo he samples, while those in captivity have accepted no fewer than nine different species. Despite their forbidding exterior bamboo-shoots make excellent eating and are served up with almost every dish wherever Chinese foregather; the plant-collector Kingdom Ward described how his men would roast the shoots by throwing them on the camp fire and then strip off the burnt outer leaves, laying bare the soft and succulent interior. Nor do the beishung restrict themselves to the shoots. Sheldon found them taking the leaves and stalks of fully mature culms up to an inch and a half in diameter, for the massive muscular development of a beishung's jaws, hinged to the deep and heavy skull, and the peculiar adaptation of his huge cheek-teeth, which are blunt grinding stumps studded with tubercles and ridges, enable him to cope with bamboo-culms that will defy the edge of the sharpest axe. As Desmond Morris has put it, 'The whole head has become modified as a crunching machine.'

No doubt the beishung prefers young succulent shoots to woody stems, if the former are available; Chi-Chi, given fresh stalks, eats the leaves first, then the stalk, but given dried bamboo takes only the thicker parts, leaving the thin pieces. Schäfer, in referring to this preference for young shoots, noted that he found no shoots in the springtime in the beishung's regular

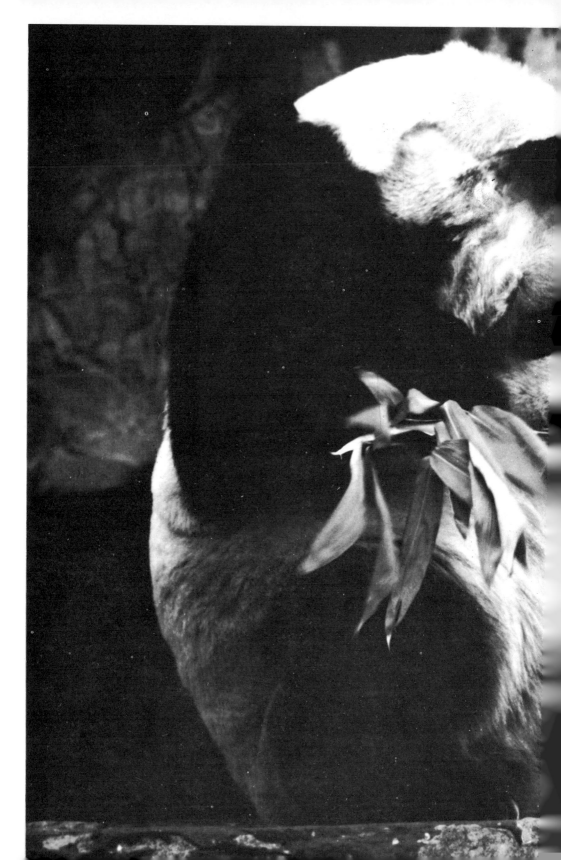

Chi-Chi inspecting bamboo.
(Russ Kinne Photo)

Chi-Chi eating bamboo in the characteristically 'human' manner. *(Zoological Society of London)*

haunts, because these had been systematically 'browsed' as they sprouted; it was his opinion that the bulk of a wild beishung's food consisted of bamboo-stems a finger or two fingers thick and as hard as a stone. With his powerful molars the beishung would bite off a section of the culm up to eighteen inches in length, at heights of from eight to sixteen inches above the ground, eat the middle portion up to the leaves but reject the harder lower portion. Feeding-places were always in the middle of the jungle, and in these fifteen or twenty stems might be found bitten off, with the rejected portions covering a square yard or two of ground.

Judging by the actions of those in captivity, the beishung feeds in extraordinarily relaxed postures, whether lying on his back or sitting upright, but in either case leaving both 'hands' free, or perhaps standing up with one forearm braced against the trunk of a tree; while Gerhard Haas describes how Chi-Chi, when chewing her bamboo, would support herself on one or both elbows at a slant above her face. Taking hold of a section of a culm with his hands the beishung carries it up to his mouth, rather than putting his mouth down to the culm, in what is superficially an extremely human manner. This he is able to do because he is equipped with a prehensile organ in the form of a working pseudo-thumb, which has been evolved from an elongated wrist-bone (the radial sesamoid), covered by a tough, rounded, fleshy pad, while the small true thumb lies passively alongside the four fingers. There has been much controversy as to the evolution and mechanism of this pseudo-thumb (which has also been developed to a lesser degree for grasping bamboo-shoots by the little panda, despite the fact that its pads are entirely covered with hair), but Desmond Morris has extracted the gist of the arguments from the mass of almost unintelligible anatomical jargon in which they are embedded. These are to the effect that this elongation of the wrist-bone acts like an opposable thumb against the fingers, but with the first two fingers pressing against the thumb, rather than the thumb against the fingers. Thus the beishung has been

equipped with a powerful forceps-type grasp, because some of the conductor muscles that would normally be attached to the true thumb have been 'taken over' by the pseudo-thumb; this is in contrast to the grasp of a bear or a racoon, whose 'fingers', aligned side by side, are closed over an object.

A beishung can therefore grasp and manipulate objects with astonishing adeptness, using one or both hands to hold his length of culm or, in captivity, sugar-cane or slice of bread; while if

The Peking cubs again, demonstrating the considerable skill of beishung in handling eating utensils. (*Eastfoto*)

uncomfortable when feeding he can raise his tin dish by gripping its side and supporting it underneath with one or both hands. Ming, when young, is reported to have used her thumb to hold a spoon and ladle up her vegetable soup; and certainly the smallest objects, such as single straws or candy-discs less than an inch in diameter, can be picked up and handled with the utmost precision.

A wild beishung, then, when feeding on bamboo, may set to work in one of two ways. He may hold the culm transversely across his mouth, as if it were a flute, and strip off the sheath of dry outer leaves quickly and neatly against the edges of his incisors; or he may push the culm into his mouth like a pipe and 'press' off the sheath between his canines and front cheek-teeth by a rotary twisting movement of his hands, coupled with a lateral movement of his head. Then, after smelling the peeled culm – or maize-stalk, celery or carrot for that matter – he pushes it slant-wise into the corner of his mouth, bites off a piece with a powerful crunch of his back molars and laboriously chews it with a succession of vertical chopping movements. But despite the thorough-ness with which he masticates the result is clearly not very efficient, because much undigested tough and fibrous material passes through his intestines. Having finished his meal he clasps his hands in front of his face and licks them and his forearms clean, and perhaps passes one licked hand across his face like a cat.

Although Schneider contended that taste plays a large part in a beishung's recognition of different species of bamboo it seems more likely that smell is the determinant sense. Chi-Chi, when on exhibition at Frankfurt, would take any food in her hands, whether birch-twigs, rye-straw or a bamboo culm, and sniff it thoroughly before she would begin to eat it, just as she would smell the hand of the keeper offering her food and also make an intensive examination of her compartment with her nose. On one occasion she was given a bundle of leeks. Holding the thick, strong-smelling bundle to her nose, she sniffed it, let it fall and trotted away; but then she returned to pick it up again, shake her head several times, lick the leeks cautiously, sniff violently and finally sit down on the bundle!

CHAPTER EIGHT
Feeding Habits

To return to Pen's interpretation of why beishung should migrate in the summer to the open steppes: it is evident that it is not at that season that they might be impelled to leave the jungle in search of food but during the winter, when only strongly woody and silicified culms are available, and much of the bamboo is heavily overlaid with snow, but when the steppes are of course inaccessible. Père David shrewdly suggested that winter conditions in the jungle would force the beishung (like the little panda) to be partly carnivorous in diet, since 'winter is a season in which

78

Chi-Chi trying her luck with the grass at London Zoo. *(Zoological Society of London)*

Red Pandas. *(Zoological Society of London)*

it is not inclined to remain asleep'.

Although W. M. Russel obtained a half-grown tame beishung, which was wandering free on a Wassu farm and apparently thriving on grass and other vegetation, it was generally supposed until quite recently that a wild beishung was as exclusively a bamboo-eater as the koala bear was thought to be exclusively tied to a diet of leaves from a single species of eucalyptus, despite the fact that it would be an extraordinary phenomenon for any animal to subsist on only one form of food through the year.

However, in 1940 Hung-shou Pen watched his Oring Nor beishung feeding on a variety of the abundant steppe plants, and probably also grubbing up roots and bulbs. He was not apparently able to identify with certainty which plants were eaten, though he implies that these included gentians, irises, crocuses, the matrimony vine and such tufted grasses as bents and rice-grass, which the Mongolian and Tibetan nomads of Tsinghai considered excellent forage for their flocks and herds.

It will be recalled that Pen's guide stated that beishung also ate pikas and fish, and more recent examinations of droppings and stomach-contents have confirmed that they do in fact frequently eat small mammals and birds; it is also reported that they have been seen scavenging the kills of other animals. It is therefore of interest that one of Chi-Chi's favourite foods is morsels of roast chicken, while An-An is provided with a cow's rib-bones with some meat attached as an addition to his daily diet of rice, milk, eggs and minerals, with birch- and aspen-twigs replacing bamboo. Chi-Chi, however, when in the Frankfurt Zoo and receiving an ample supply of bamboo-culms and fresh rice-straw, showed little liking for birch-twigs, tending to play with them rather than eat them.

In 1915 a description was published of the well-preserved skull of a prehistoric beishung that had been found in a cave in the fabulous ruby mines at Mogok, on a tributary of the upper

Irrawaddy, some four hundred miles to the south-west of the present known range of *Ailuropoda melanoleuca*. It is interesting to note that this prehistoric beishung, which lived in the Pleistocene era – some four hundred million years ago according to the most recent estimates – was equipped with canines that were considerably longer and stouter than those of our beishung, large though these are for an animal that is mainly a vegetarian. Moreover, its pre-molars, lying just behind the canines, were not only smaller than a beishung's but defective. Since the latter arrangement is common to the great cats, increasing the penetrative efficiency of the canines when making a kill, one may deduce that the beishung's ancestors were partly predatory.

According to B. H. Hodgson of the Indian Civil Service, who discovered more about the habits of the *wáh*s (as the lesser pandas were known to the hill peoples of Sikkim, because of their child-like cries) in the early nineteenth century than anyone appears to have done since, these little pandas are not in fact generally carnivorous:

> I have had many brought to me [he wrote], and have kept several for a year or two in Nepal, feeding them on rice and milk or milk only, or eggs, all of which they like, though they wholly refuse rats, fish, insects, snakes, and rarely and reluctantly take flesh of any kind. I have often put a small live fowl into their cage, but seldom knew them kill and never eat it, though if it approached them too nearly they would rush at it and give it a severe and possibly fatal blow with the forepaws. But they love milk and *ghee,* and constantly make their way furtively into remote dairies and cowherds' cottages to possess themselves of these luxuries.

Although equipped with the same broad bamboo-crunching molars as the beishung, the little panda is certainly omnivorous, feeding not only on bamboo-shoots but also on such varied items as tuberous roots, acorns, beech-mast, leaves, fruits and birds' eggs; and though a good climber, sleeping for most of the day in the topmost branches of conifers, it feeds mainly on the ground in the early morning and late evening, and also rears its two young at ground level in rock crevices.

What a wild-born animal can be induced to eat in captivity is of course no indication that similar foods would be taken in the natural state, but captive beishung enjoy and thrive on a wide variety of foods – young willow-twigs, green maize-stalks, celery-stalks, lettuce, carrots, potatoes, apples, pears, oranges, bananas, oat-flakes, bread, spaghetti, blackcurrant jam and sugar – preferring soft foods in mash or porridge form. In her young days Chi-Chi would also drink fresh water several times a day in long draughts, without apparently making use of her tongue; but wild beishung may never actually drink water, since the bamboo jungle is perpetually moist with rain, cloud and mist.

In this respect it is perhaps significant that Tangier Smith's five beishung refused to drink water when they arrived at the Kowloon Dogs' Home, though they must have been excessively dehydrated after three weeks in transit from Szechwan, but accepted well-watered milk.

At first [wrote Rosa Loseby] they were suspicious of condensed milk when I offered them a tin with the usual small holes. However, after a few minutes, each one realised that it was something really worth having. The 'baby' [Ming] quickly learned to pick up the tin and roll on her back, in which position she remained until the tin was taken away. A tin of milk was the only thing which would arouse the oldest, whom we called 'Grandma' [who died in London of double pneumonia the following January]. The tin would last her for three hours, the greater part of which was spent in licking the milk from her hair, on which it had spouted when she gave the tin a crunch.

Ivor Montagu has suggested that beishung may be wary of approaching water, in view of the fact that this is represented in Hsi-fan by mountain torrents and deep lakes large enough to be described as inland seas. But in fact their trails through the bamboo-thickets lead down to and across watercourses, and Sheldon records an instance of one beishung crossing a stream sixteen feet wide in order to reach a burnt clearing where young bamboo-shoots were springing up. It is true, however, that beishung in captivity make no attempt to bathe, and seldom

paddle in the swimming-pools or fish-ponds in their quarters, despite the fact that they are often subjected to unnaturally high temperatures. But Chi-Chi, for one, much enjoys a bubble-bath, while a shower or mist-spray, which she no doubt regards as a natural form of rain, together with large blocks of ice for her to lie on, is provided in the summer at Regent's Park. In her earlier days at Frankfurt she bathed willingly in a tub, sitting upright and splashing with pleasure, gathering up quantities of water with both hands and rubbing it on her face, before climbing out of the tub after five minutes or so, shaking herself several times and trotting off across the grass.

84

Not all beishung dislike water – Chi-Chi enjoying a bubble-bath at Frankfurt.
(Tierbilder Okapia)

We still have not answered the question of why some beishung should repair to the open steppe during the summer months, nor is it clear how near these Tsinghai steppes lie to inhabited jungles; but one assumes that these visits are made not because bamboo-culms are unavailable at this season but merely for a change to vegetable and perhaps animal diet. Weather conditions may be an influential factor. An animal with extremely dense woolly hair, lying long and close and two inches or more thick in places, and a slightly oily, very thick undercoat does not voluntarily tolerate heat; and within the bamboo-zone the beishung will certainly go higher in hot weather and lower in cold. Caroline

Jarvis noted that in the Peking and Shanghai zoos, where the beishung are housed behind glass in air-conditioned cages furnished with rocks, pools and water-sprays to freshen the bamboo, they passed the heat of the day indoors; but in the morning and evening, when it was cooler, they would go into their grassy enclosures to wander among the clumps of bamboo and mimosa trees. Although Schäfer encountered one beishung rolling on its back on an open stretch of grass in the early morning, Sage and Sheldon were led to believe by their tracks that they were mainly nocturnal in their movements, 'wandering and feeding along ridge sides from one bamboo thicket to another, and when day came, lying up to sleep in a den among the ledges or in a warm spot in the sun'; and the general consensus of opinion is that, while they do some feeding very early in the morning and late in the evening, the bulk of their food is taken during the night. But a beishung is not specially equipped to see in the dark, and cannot be presumed to select and manipulate his culms solely by touch and smell. Conditions in captivity, where ample food is always available and no time or energy need be spent in searching for it, cannot be compared with those prevailing in the wild; but Chi-Chi, after being given her breakfast at eight o'clock, sleeps for a short time after her midday lunch and also rests again during the middle of the night, while Happy was not only accustomed to rest a great deal during the day but, as evening approached, would run (in so far as a beishung can run) to his straw hut as soon as this was opened up, and quickly fall asleep.

It is much more probable that a wild beishung is neither specifically nocturnal nor specifically diurnal, but feeds whenever conditions are suitable, taking advantage no doubt of clear and moonlit nights; for there is no questioning the fact that, if a beishung has only to stretch out his hand to reach a culm of bamboo, he has nevertheless to work long hours in order to obtain an adequate supply of bulk food, because of the extraordinary rapidity of his digestive processes. Tangier Smith's description of the beishung as 'the laziest animal in the world', obtaining its food with the minimum of active effort, coupled with the enervation displayed by those in captivity at sea-level, perhaps ten thousand feet below their natural habitat, has created a totally false impression. Wild beishung are, as we have seen, continually on the move, forcing passages through the bamboo-thickets, migrating from one wood to another, scrambling up and down precipitous hillsides. And it is evident that they can negotiate this difficult country much more expeditiously than their lumbering gait would suggest. Weigold, who accompanied the Wassu on several extremely arduous hunts over the roughest country and along the tunnel-like trails that penetrated the dense thickets, was never able to get closer to one than the sight of rustling bushes closing behind his quarry on the far side of a small opening in the thicket.

A beishung is known to consume as much as twenty pounds of culms and leaves in a day, and Sheldon estimated that one would have to feed for ten or twelve hours a day out of the twenty-four to satisfy his requirements, for the culms pass almost undigested straight through his stomach, which retains little of their nutritive goodness. Moreover, large quantities of culms are not even swallowed, but merely chewed; and these waste-products, together with the droppings, are to be found all along the beishung's trails. Indeed, the extraordinary number of droppings deposited by a single beishung, often in large heaps after the manner of a rhinoceros, not only along the trail but also in and around his sleeping-places, inevitably leads the observer into supposing that more beishung are present in a particular jungle than is in fact the case or, alternatively, that they remain in the same locality for longer periods than they actually do.

Sheldon made some observations on this aspect of the beishung's daily routine. At nine o'clock on the morning of 15 November, for instance, when four inches of snow were covering the ground, Sheldon picked up a beishung track high on a mountain slope to the south of Chengwai. The beishung had emerged from very dense bamboo jungle lower on the slope, and was on its way to a mixed forest of bamboo and spruce higher up.

Snow had fallen during the night, and the track obviously had been made early that morning. For two miles it wound in and out through the bamboo thickets where the animal had fed, and the surprising detail was that at an average of every hundred yards there were from one to three large droppings (4 to 6 inches long and one to two inches thick, tapering at

each end). At a conservative estimate there were forty droppings, when the track was still two hours old. At this point I
disturbed the panda, but could not see it because of the dense
bamboo. The animal had been resting at the base of a small
spruce tree, and must have stopped feeding before 9 a.m. On
his trail he had stopped occasionally to feed, but there was
every reason to believe that the bulk of his meal had been
obtained below the point at which I encountered the tracks.
This instance led me to believe that the giant panda often feeds
at night (as do several other large mammals of the region). I
pursued this particular animal for three hours longer, and I
found droppings almost as frequently for another four miles,
although it had not stopped to feed meanwhile.

CHAPTER NINE

Mating and Disposition

Natives and Westerners alike agree that beishung are solitary in their habits. Schäfer suggested that every beishung has its own territory of not less than a square kilometre in area, and Sheldon that a single animal probably confines its range to one main valley, with each panda 'making the rounds', so to speak, about once a week. This is an interesting suggestion, because making the rounds of a territory is a habit shared by so many mammals, whether carnivorous or herbivorous. The beishung's habits of stretching up on his hind legs to a height of five feet or so and scoring his sharp, hooked claws down the bark of large trees and also of rubbing himself against those trees are possibly for the purpose of indicating territorial boundaries rather than for paring away the jagged edges on his claws, since, unlike the big cats, he has no great need to keep his claws in impeccable trim for hunting purposes, though, in contrast to those of the little panda, they are fully retractable.

Although Sage and Sheldon were informed that some beishung lived in pairs, and a farmer in the Chengwai valley told them that two would occasionally come down into the valley together, the general hearsay is that it is only during the mating that two or more adults are to be seen together. The mating is usually reported to be in April, though in captivity both Chi-Chi and An-An have been on heat for spells of from ten days to three weeks from February to April or May and again, significantly, to a lesser degree in the autumn. Since in neither case were these climacterics able to fulfil their natural functions they cannot be taken as necessarily applicable to wild beishung, any more than can the gestation periods of captives. However, Li-Li's first cub, Ming-Ming, was born on 9 September, after 148 days' gestation, and her twins (which may have been premature) on 4 September, after 120 days. These periods would imply matings during the third week in April and the first week in May respectively. But either the mating season or gestation period is different in the wild state or, as in the case of so many mammals, including the bears, there may be a delay in the implantation of the ovary, for the majority of wild cubs on which data is available have been born in the period November to February, which implies that mating took place between June and early September. Chi-Chi and the Bronx Zoo's Pan were almost certainly born in June, indicating a mating about the middle of January.

Contact between the sexes at the approach of the mating season will almost certainly be by scent, for a feature of the in-heat season of both female and male in captivity is their scent-marking procedure. Happy, for example, would rub his hind-parts against any upright object, such as a branch, and urinate a little; while Chi-Chi, according to Desmond Morris, passes a great deal of her time rubbing her swollen vulva on the ground, and frequently backs up to special rubbing-points in her enclosure,

An-An scent marking. *(Zoological Society of London)*

lowers her head, hollows her back and, raising her tail, rubs her ano-genital region on the hard surface. This action deposits sticky glandular secretions, which leave a strong personal scent, and is associated with a powerful shaking and tossing of her head and often with an open-mouthed grin. Of particular interest to us in attempting to reconstruct the behaviour of wild beishung is the fact that Chi-Chi resorts to the same scenting-places not only day after day but also from one year to the next. That she does so may merely indicate the possession of a retentive memory, but it could equally well be that her scent endures for an indefinite period. Nor is scent-marking restricted only to the season of 'heat', for it may also occur during a captive beishung's daily patrol around its enclosure.

In the wild state fighting is reported during the mating season, possibly as a preliminary to successful coupling, and females in heat certainly become rather aggressive. At this time both sexes bleat like sheep, while according to Brocklehurst the male utters a kind of roar similar to but more prolonged than the 'sawing' cough of a leopard. This he is reported to do for three or four days in succession. Possibly this period of roaring serves the purpose of establishing one male's proprietary rights to the female, because the natives say that the latter ensconces herself in a tree at this time, while the male remains on the ground, presumably guarding her from the attentions of other males in the vicinity. However that may be, captive males certainly run around, barking, a great deal during the mating season.

In the ordinary course of events the beishung is not a very vociferous animal. He may snort in anger or, when young, squeak when his dish is filled with food or when being scratched by his keeper; but his most characteristic vocal expression, whether it be when the keeper appears with bamboo or water-bucket, or when flies plague him, or when he wishes to retire in the evening to his sleeping-place, is a teeth-clattering, comparable to the mouth-clapping of a brown bear. This sound is produced by a rhythmical and repeated striking together of lower and upper jaws, from which the lips are withdrawn, exposing his front teeth; and indeed he clatters as if he were equipped with false teeth.

During the mating season both sexes go off their food when in captivity. Desmond Morris writes of Chi-Chi:

> When she became mature and started to experience her first periods of heat, it was the porridge and not the bamboo that fell out of favour. Previously she had been only too eager to demolish her special mixture and, as with other pandas, she was in danger of becoming de-bambooed. But now, with her food-intake sinking lower and lower as the sexual mood increased, it was the porridge that was the first to be ignored. At the height of the sexual heat, nothing at all was eaten, but just before and after the heat she would still toy with a branch of bamboo shoots.

During her second heat she would eat only the tenderest bamboos.

Since the genital organs of immature beishung, both male and female, are covered with thick skin beneath very long fur, it has proved very difficult to determine the sex of captive specimens. The male's organs do not become visible until he is five or six years old, and Chi-Chi's sex was still undetermined in 1963 when she was seven years old. According to Chinese zoologists, however, an immature beishung's sex can be judged by its habits and disposition, since females tend to be gentler and more sociable while males are ill-tempered and inclined to be moody and easily angered. Indeed, Mei-Lan, the Brookfield Zoo's male, mauled a keeper's arm so severely that it had to be amputated. But when Chi-Chi had just terminated a week's heat at the age of seven, for the first time since her cub days she suddenly attacked her keeper (who had only been in charge of her for a few weeks) and, knocking him down, sat on him and savaged his leg. However, since she had by then experienced four years of frustrated 'heats' without a male, such an upset was likely to occur sooner or later.

Moroseness is the classic malady of many captive animals, especially those in solitary confinement, as has been the lot of most beishung, and so cannot be considered necessarily characteristic of their kind or sex; and Morris doubts whether these Chinese clues to sexual distinction are valid. On the other hand a stock-breeder or field naturalist would suppose that typical differences in behaviour, particularly of the male, would be apparent long before adulthood. This, if size be the criterion, is reached when the beishung is five or six years old, though Chi-Chi's first heat did in fact occur when she was three and a half. If beishung are indeed this slow in maturing they may well live to a ripe old age of twenty-five or thirty years. The ages of those in captivity do not at present indicate their potential life-span, for although Chi-Chi is in good health in her thirteenth year the oldest of all zoo beishung, Mei-Lan, died at the age of fourteen years and eight months, probably from some intestinal trouble since he was very emaciated at death, weighing only 205 pounds, while the next oldest, Pao-Pei, who was purchased from a German dealer by the St Louis Zoo as a mate for Happy, died at thirteen and a half.

Although beishung have been depicted as placid beasts in the main their moods are as variable as their 'personalities'. Ruth Harkness noted that the young Su-Lin was subject to sudden likes and dislikes (which she believed to originate in his marvellous sense of smell); and Schneider, believing him to be a female, wrote of Happy: 'One saw on several occasions how, when one came too close, she would swiftly turn and go over to the attack. This apparently harmless, dreamy creature, at whose behaviour one could only smile, suddenly became a predator again'; whereas with those he knew he was very trusting, and the keeper in charge could pick him up without hindrance and gently scratch and tickle him. So too Chi-Chi, on being transferred after a month or two from Frankfurt to London, treated her new keepers with reserve, or even chased them, until she became accustomed to them. Su-Lin, Happy and Chi-Chi represent the happy personalities of their kind; Lien-Ho, who passed most of her four years at Regent's Park hiding among the roof-struts of her cage, the moody type.

CHAPTER TEN
Chi-Chi and An-An

Li-Li, although on very affectionate terms with her first mate, had no cubs until the arrival of a second mate, Pi-Pi, in 1962, after the latter had been confined to a 'husbandry station' – whatever that may imply – for three years. A major problem in mating captive animals that have been kept in solitary confinement is that they may have become 'imprinted' to prefer humans to those of their own kind. In this respect, consider the affair of Chi-Chi and An-An.

It was in March 1966, when she was rising nine years old, that

Chi-Chi was flown to Moscow, in the hope that she would mate with An-An, then eight years old, when she came into season in the autumn. The two were housed in adjacent compartments with a sliding grille between them. When they were first allowed out together in a covered open-air paddock An-An behaved in an appropriately masculine manner, but, since Chi-Chi was not then in 'heat', behaved so aggressively towards this intruder in his 'territory' that the two had thereafter to be confined to their own quarters. This behaviour confirms reports that in the wild state male and female beishung maintain separate territories except during the mating season.

As it happened it was the end of September before Chi-Chi began her autumnal heat. On 1 October she did not eat up her food with her customary enthusiasm, and two mornings later, after refusing her breakfast, she approached the dividing grille; but then – only too significantly, in the light of subsequent events – instead of attempting to attract An-An she moved away to the bars of her own cage and presented her rump to the keeper. However, the moment of truth was at hand, and Moscow cabled to London: URGENT YOU PRESENT – or whatever the Russian idiom for that may be.

Desmond Morris, together with Michael Lyster, the Zoological Society's photographer, and other members of the Regent's Park staff, flew to Moscow the next day, when Chi-Chi was again soliciting the keeper and An-An, sensing a change in the affairs of pandas, had begun to bleat amorously. On the following morning Chi-Chi was soliciting An-An, pressing her rump against the grille and bleating; while he for his part showed a proper curiosity at such an invitation, sniffing at her with interest. The London contingent requested immedite action, but this was not considered feasible by the Russians, in view of the various preparations to be made and precautions to be taken before a meeting between the two could be safely arranged; and it was agreed that this should be fixed for the following afternoon when Sosnovsky – Morris's counterpart – had returned from Budapest. But in the meantime the two pandas were allowed separately into the larger open-air enclosure, in which they had first met the previous March, in order that they might be filmed and their behaviour studied.

After her six months' acclimatization Chi-Chi, who had put on weight during her stay in Moscow, appeared as fully relaxed as only a panda can be, lying on her back full-length on the straw bales that had been strewn over what had originally been a rock-pool, with her arms behind her head and legs curved out in luxurious abandon – though subsequent events were anything but relaxed! Some months later I was able to see Lyster's striking colour film of the meeting between Chi-Chi and An-An, which highlighted not only the dramatic contrast between glossy black and white but also the surprising grace of movement, with the whole length of foreleg and inward-curving paw set down with stealthily attractive deliberation, as they walked slowly around the enclosure, sniffing here and there. An-An subsequently bounced playfully across the paddock and rubbed his backside on the concrete at the edge of the 'pool', leaving a dark scent-mark.

6 October. Moscow Zoo is closed to the public after 1.0 p.m. At 3.0 p.m. a riot-squad with water-hose, wooden shields and anaesthetic pistol stands by to separate the two pandas in the event of serious fighting; and a few minutes later Chi-Chi is allowed into the open-air enclosure. She enters very cautiously, possibly because there is a strong scent of An-An about. An attempt is then made to introduce the latter into the enclosure, when Chi-Chi has moved down to the 'pool' at some distance from An-An's grille; but as soon as she hears the grille being opened she runs across to it and it has to be shut to prevent her entering his private compartment. After a repetition of this it is finally possible to admit An-An into the enclosure. He immediately picks up her scent and chases her, as she shambles away from him, apparently frightened. With Chi-Chi barking ferociously, and both striking out with their forepaws, they scrap briefly, though without either making any serious attempt to bite the other – not that one would have expected them to, for what bite could penetrate a beishung's immensely thick coat and underlying fat? Subsequently An-An (with a curious, bleeping call, which can only be transcribed as a kind of yodelling trill) repeatedly pursues Chi-Chi around the rock-pool with lumbering chases and two or three attempted mountings, but as invariably retreats when she barks and snaps at him and cuffs him with her

Chi-Chi watches An-An.
An-An watches Chi-Chi . . .

. . . chases her . . .
. . . and gets his ears boxed.
(Zoological Society of London)

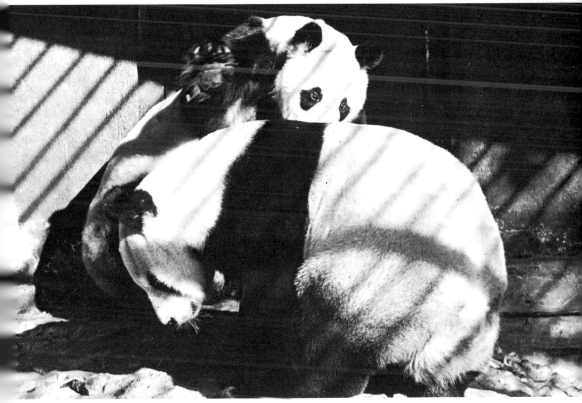

paw. Her actions are those of an animal that does not understand
what this other animal is attempting to do; while An-An is
extraordinarily and unnaturally timid in his advances, backing
away and lumbering off immediately she turns on him, without
ever attempting to hold his ground or to retaliate in any way after
their initial encounter. And when he does eventually catch up
with her and succeed in mounting he is unable to achieve an
erection, while she keeps her tail firmly and discouragingly down.
Indeed, after an hour of these abortive chases, Chi-Chi is so
upset that she has diarrhoea while swaying and weaving in front
of her grille in that stereotyped manner normally associated with
an animal that has spent a long period in captivity, and scratching
at it in an attempt to get away from An-An and back to the privacy
of her own compartment; while he stretches out on the straw
bales, rolling around on his back, pulling at the bales and tearing
them to pieces in frustration.

The following day there were two 'mating' sessions. The morning one followed the same pattern as that of their first meeting,
except that there was no fighting; but in the afternoon Chi-Chi
began to be deliberately aggressive towards An-An, and though
she did no more than bark and swipe at him he was again so
surprisingly unmasculine as to run away from these mild on-
slaughts. In these circumstances the obvious course was to leave
the two together all night, in the hope that they might settle down.
Both slept during the late evening, but after this rest Chi-Chi
paced to and fro for several hours – resolving this new problem in
her life? Most unlikely! Just pacing, restless at this break in
normal routine, for she had eaten very little during the past six
days. However, proximity to Chi-Chi throughout the night did
stimulate An-An, and at dawn he made a real attempt to mate
with her, seizing her by the scruff of the neck and holding her
down; but though he now achieved an erection, Chi-Chi
thwarted him by refusing to raise her tail, and subsequently drove
him off with another bout of paw-swiping and barking. At 10.45
a.m. the mating sponsors admitted temporary defeat and the
contrary pair were removed to their respective compartments for
a meal – which An-An accepted but Chi-Chi again refused. It
was now determined that they should rest for the remainder of
the day, before being put together again for the night.

When the time came for their fourth meeting at 5.0 p.m. Chi-Chi objected strongly to being driven out of her compartment, roaring violently, and roaring again on seeing An-An. However, she soon quietened down, and the remainder of the evening was passed in sleep, with occasional periods of mild activity when one approached the other. But nothing of moment occurred during the night, and the two were separated once again at 7.0 a.m. – when Chi-Chi proceeded to solicit the exasperated and unresponsive human observers!

9 October. An-An is now eating well, while Chi-Chi also takes a little food; and at 5.30 p.m. a fifth session is arranged. But it is now difficult to persuade Chi-Chi to leave her compartment. Instead, she repeatedly presents her rump to the observers, accompanying this with a new form of bleat, differing from An-An's; carrying her soliciting to such lengths that, on the keeper's entering her compartment in order to push her out with a wooden screen, and patting her back, she raises her tail and rump invitingly in response to the pressure of his hand! But when after an hour's struggle she is finally persuaded to enter the mating enclosure she barks loudly at An-An and refuses to allow him near her, although he is still fully interested in her. By the evening both are asleep, and although An-An approaches her a number of times during the early morning, and once touches her back, she rejects his advances on every occasion.

With the failure of this fifth mating attempt new tactics were called for, and it was agreed that the two should be kept apart for thirty-six hours. However, on the evening of the 11th Sosnovsky was of the opinion that it was too cold for the pandas to be left outside all night, and their meeting was delayed until 5.0 a.m. the next morning. But at 9.30 a.m. Chi-Chi was still in her own compartment, despite four and a half hours of 'intensive persuasion' aimed at driving her out to meet An-An, and despite the fact that she was posturing sexually to the human observers. Mating attempt number six was now abandoned; but on this occasion Chi-Chi's grille to the outer paddock was left open, and at 4.0 p.m. she emerged of her own accord and the grille was closed behind her. But when An-An was allowed into the paddock half an hour later there was no improvement in her attitude towards him after their two-day separation. Barking at him, she repeatedly

Chi-Chi 'soliciting' a human at Moscow. (*Zoological Society of London*)

drove him away – and this despite the fact that at one stage, when he was only ten feet from her, she responded sexually with raised tail to the presence of a human hand on her back (through the bars of the cage) and orientated towards the latter, only to abandon her posturing and move away when An-An came closer! After several repetitions of this provoking behaviour this abortive meeting was terminated at 6.30 p.m.

The following evening an eighth attempt was made, but abandoned after half an hour, since Chi-Chi stubbornly refused to leave her compartment; and she was then left to rest for the night, in preparation for her flight home to London.

That this attempt to mate two captive giant pandas should have failed after some sixty hours' contact was not (at any rate with hindsight) unexpected, despite their six months' proximity; and it would probably be unfair to suggest that a successful mating might have been achieved could human observation, with its inevitably distracting accompanying paraphernalia of lighting, camera and sound-recording apparatus, minimal though it was, have been cut out. After their first autumnal encounter it was thought that Chi-Chi's sexuality might have been depressed by the shock of their meeting, and also by actual fear of An-An. But their behaviour at subsequent meetings demonstrated that, after several years of total separation from animals of her own kind, Chi-Chi in particular had become humanized or imprinted in favour of humans rather than pandas; while An-An also displayed what one would suppose to be an unnatural timidity towards her, together with an unmasculine lack of determination in his attempts to force a mating, despite his original aggressiveness towards her when they had first met in March, when she was not in season. Whether their age and physical condition contributed to their failure to mate cannot be determined, though it must be considered significant that six years had elapsed since Chi-Chi's first heat. An-An was, perhaps naturally, distressed, panting heavily and frothing at the mouth, after his chases and abortive mountings; and both appeared to be too fat; but a beishung is a much larger animal than one might suppose, with a full-grown male measuring five or six feet from nose to rump, and one presumes that even a wild beishung must always appear fat because of his roly-poly figure and extraordinarily dense coat. In actual fact Chi-Chi, at 235 pounds, was believed to be of average weight for a female and was not to be compared with Pan-Dah, who reached the extraordinary weight for a female of 379 pounds during her ten years of apparent good health in the Bronx Zoo. At 339 pounds An-An was believed to be some forty pounds above the average weight for a male; but the maximum size of a beishung may have been underestimated. Ping-Ping, another Moscow male, who was almost certainly less than seven years old when he died and therefore only just in his prime, reached a weight of 399 pounds. Because neither An-An nor Ping-Ping was fed any of his natural food, bamboo, it has been generally assumed that both were overweight; and since captive animals are also usually underexercised this is a reasonable assumption. Nevertheless both Brocklehurst and Tangier Smith refer to four-hundred-pound wild males.

Whatever may have been the precise reasons for Chi-Chi's and An-An's failure to mate it was agreed at the conclusion of the unsuccessful 1966 meeting that artificial insemination would be too hazardous an operation to be employed with such rare animals, but that, though the prospects of a normal mating in different circumstances were very slight, this might be achieved by taking An-An to London the following year for a protracted visit from February to November. This extended period would cover both seasons of sexual activity, while such prolonged contact between the two pandas in the larger enclosures available at Regent's Park might possibly result in Chi-Chi's affections being redirected to her own kind. Sosnovsky emphasized, however, that such a project would require official sanction; and in the event Moscow Zoo announced early in 1967 that An-An was suffering a series of stomach upsets, and was not in a fit state to visit London. However, An-An did in fact visit London in the autumn of 1968, though one felt that the chances of a successful mating would be remote after the lapse of so many sterile years. And this, unhappily, proved to be the case, although An-An stayed at Regent's Park until late in the following spring.

CHAPTER ELEVEN

Young Beishung

From the little evidence available it would seem that a beishung gives birth to one cub more often than two, though she possesses two pairs of nipples, pectoral and abdominal. According to native reports, the young are born in the typical sleeping-places of the adult – at the base of a tree or under a dead stump, in crevices in rock ledges and often under overhanging rocks on precipitous slopes, but evidently especially in hollow trees. Sheldon saw a well-used 'nest' on top of a large, flat stump in an opening in the bamboo jungle, and Schäfer observed that in one territory many well-used paths led to bamboo-thickets, tree-stumps and tunnel-like hollows, all of which were regularly slept in; but these were not near the feeding-places in the denser thickets. Sleeping-places on the ground were in hollows furnished with leaves scraped together and broken bits of culms carried to them from a distance and arranged to form a nest. No doubt a beishung is not very particular as to how he sleeps. An-An can be seen snoring while lying with his rear parts on a step and his head cuddled on his left paw at a lower elevation; and the young Chi-Chi would sleep on her back or side with one arm over her eyes, possibly to shade them from the light. That by placing a black paw over her white face she may camouflage her presence from the hungry eyes of a leopard or bird of prey, as Schneider has suggested, seems a far-fetched explanation.

It is generally believed today that beishung do not hibernate, and they certainly do not den up for six or seven months in hollow trees and caves as Wilson was told by the natives, for they are abroad in the first days of March and raiding the farmers' bee-hives. On the other hand Pen, who subsequently made a five-month expedition to Minya Konka in western Szechwan in 1962, reports (cryptically) finding an earthen cave in which a beishung had wintered before moving in the summer months to sunken ground covered with moss and grass; and although Weigold saw fresh droppings of chewed-up culms on the snow early in January, and Brocklehurst stated that he had seen the 'forms' of beishung in the snow on several occasions, there is no actual evidence that they may not den up for short periods at midwinter, when heavy snowfalls render it difficult for them to negotiate the bamboo-thickets in search of food.

Moreover, the majority of beishung cubs are almost certainly born between November and February, when conditions in the high bamboo jungles are very severe. Weighing only four or five ounces at birth, the cubs must obviously remain holed up and in need of their mother's warmth for several weeks, despite their thick, brownish-black and white guard-hair and soft, grey-brown belly fur. They must also be very frequently suckled, because within ten weeks (at which age they are cutting their first milk-teeth) their weight has increased twenty-five- or thirty-fold. In this connection Li-Li is reported to have neither eaten nor slept

Li-Li cuddling the baby Ming-Ming *(Tierbilder Okapia) (Eastfoto)*

107

Ming-Ming begins to find his feet, and Li-Li gets back into the beishung's daily routine. *(World Wildlife Fund)*

for the first few days after the birth of Ming-Ming, holding her tightly clasped in her forepaws throughout this period and for the next few weeks continuing to cradle her gently against her chest, fondling her in a startlingly human manner, while sitting with her back against a corner of the pen. When the cub was two months old she would play with it by tossing it from one arm to the other, and if the cub was impatient she would soothe it with her paw, like a mother caressing her child. So too she cradled Lin-Lin, her second cub, continuously for the first ten days after birth, even when she was eating. Furthermore, the cub can only crawl or roll around for the first three months; and only then, when it is about thirty inches in length and twelve or thirteen pounds in weight, will a captive cub frequently wander away from its mother when

'An infinite capacity for
relaxing with bamboo-stalks.'
(Russ Kinne)

she is sleeping. In the light of these facts, would it be practicable for a wild cub to leave its hollow-tree 'nest' or cave before it could accompany its mother? The breeding females, then, may well go into partial hibernation for periods of days or weeks, while the males, with no parental responsibilities, continue to move around, as male polar bears do when the females are lying up in their snow dens.

Ming-Ming was weaned at the age of six months, when she weighed twenty-five to thirty pounds, onto a thrice-daily diet of milk, rice and eggs, fortified with vitamins, bone-meal, salt and liver-oil; but she was a year old and eighty pounds in weight before she began to sample bamboo, a couple of months before her first permanent teeth began to come through. Thereafter a cub reaches 120 pounds by the age of sixteen months, and is, as we have seen, full grown between five and six years old. Size is the most obvious distinction between the sexes, though there is also a slight contrast in colour, with the female's white markings appearing brighter than the male's because of the finer texture of her fur and because the male's black markings are rather more extensive. In some specimens, and notably those of an adult and an immature female obtained by Weigold and the female shot by Sage, the white parts on the back display a pronounced yellowish or even reddish tint.

Life in the wild state for a young beishung is no doubt very different from that in captivity, even if a wild cub has less to fear from predators than most young mammals. In captivity the cubs are active and playful, tumbling about during most of their waking hours, though with an infinite capacity for relaxing with bamboo-stalks when a little older. 'There lay the young rascal in the sun,' wrote Schneider of Happy, 'astride or as in an armchair, with limbs hanging or with head on one arm. But it was also able to rest on the ground: on its belly with hind legs stretched out and its head on crooked arm, or on its back with feet in the air.' John Tee-Van, who made a round trip of some thirty thousand miles to collect Pan-Dah and Pan-Dee from Dr Graham and transport them back to the Bronx Zoo, stresses this aspect of the beishung's character when he describes his first sight of Pan-Dah. 'Sitting on her haunches, with paw-supported chin resting on the arm of a wooden swing, was a sleepy-faced panda calmly contemplating

114

Gymnastics at Frankfurt. *(Gerhard Haas)*

a small brick-walled world.' Chi-Chi, when a cub, much enjoyed swinging on a spring-balance from which the mechanism had been removed, although she regarded it with immense suspicion initially, venturing onto it only after considerable encouragement.

Although beishung become much less active as they mature

115

they remain playful for an unusually long time. Chi-Chi, when
five years old, was still wrestling with her rubber bucket, swinging
on a suspended motor-tyre, standing on her head or playing
tug-o'-war with her keeper; while Schneider describes the
three- or four-year-old Happy as having an instinctive impulse to
play like a child: thrashing about in his straw bedding and busying
himself with his own limbs; pulling straw over his head like
ribbons; blowing sawdust off the floor with his nose; rolling over
on his back while trying to bite his tail through his legs. He would
experiment with every imaginable posture – standing on his head
near the bars of his cage, and righting himself with a somersault;
sitting on the rim of a motor-tyre, or inside it, and then flinging
himself backwards out of it; setting it on edge and pushing his
head through the hole, and then hanging it round his neck or
sprawling right through it, and trying the same manœuvre backwards; pushing the tyre over his body, as if he were sitting in a
lifebelt, and then lying down on his back and using his hind legs
to grip the tyre and crawl through it.

Despite his massive compactness and clumsy gait an outstanding feature of the beishung's physique is the remarkable suppleness of his limbs and body. Whether sitting or lying he can scratch
almost every part of his body. He can reach his shoulders or his
head behind his ears with hands or feet, or thrust a back leg
straight up, while in a sitting position, and rest his chin on it. He
sits characteristically leaning back against a support, even if this
be no more substantial than an iron stake, with legs stretched out
and the soles of his feet turned up, and head thrown back so that
he can contemplate at ease the wonders of Nature. Gerhard Haas
has described how the young Chi-Chi, at the Frankfurt Zoo,
would sometimes fasten both hands under her knees and rock
herself to and fro on her back. She would also stand on her head
for lengthy periods, while leaning against a tree-stump or the
wire of her cage, or freely in the middle of the cage, and often
come out of her headstand in a somersault; or, with her feet
against the wire, would 'run' along on her hands. When head-
standing thirty inches above the ground on a fork of her tree she
would rest her arms on the two forks and then raise her body and
legs on high and hold this position for several minutes, before
allowing herself to fall to the ground.

116

CHAPTER TWELVE

Numbers and Range

The giant panda has been adopted as its symbol by the World Wildlife Fund, which is responsible for the preservation and conservation of the world's rapidly declining stocks of wildlife. How scarce are giant pandas? It is perhaps worth recalling in this context that previously mentioned gift of seventy white bear-skins, together with two live white bears, which the Emperor of China is reported to have presented to the Tenno of Japan in the year 685. So large a gift of skins of what, from the restricted nature of its habitat and its solitary habits, can never have been an excessively numerous animal does pose the question of whether these were in fact the skins of beishung. Some sceptics have wondered whether they were not those of polar bears, which had previously been mentioned in the Japanese Imperial annals for 658, and whose skins were prized possessions of the Tartar nomads in later centuries. But it seems even more unlikely that a Chinese emperor would have had so many polar-bear skins in his possession, while according to Herbert Wendt all the old Chinese records stated that the skins of these 'white bears' had black markings on them.

However that may be, when Ruth Harkness, the amateur of amateurs, captured two cubs on her second expedition, and Tangier Smith followed her west almost immediately with no fewer than five live beishung, it became evident that previous reports of their scarcity had been exaggerated. The Roosevelts in particular had confused the issue with their insistence that few of the peasant farmers and villagers whom they encountered in Hsi-fan were aware of the existence of beishung in the forests above their valleys. Those in the villages around Tatsienlu, for instance, believed the explorers to be referring to the brown or 'red' bear when they inquired about the beishung; while ten out of thirteen hunters at Luchinga, where the Roosevelts found moderately fresh traces and were given a skin, declared that they had never seen a live beishung, despite the fact that two had been killed there in the previous nine years. So too at Tachow, twenty-five miles from Yehli, the magistrate and his companions had never heard of such an animal, and did not recognize a picture of one. This one can believe, because Chinese officials had no interest in any matters except local gossip, and only the merchants and traders fraternized easily with foreigners. At Bedung, however, some eighty miles west of Yehli, neither the native Chinese nor the aboriginal Lo-Los recognized a picture of one, nor had they ever seen a skin. Clearly, there was a deliberate or unwitting blockage in communication between the Roosevelt party and the villagers and hunters they questioned. No other Westerners confirm this native ignorance of beishung, and it is inconceivable that the Lo-Lo aboriginals would not know it. Yet those at Yehli are reported by the Roosevelts to have stated not only that beishung were exceedingly rare but that the specimen shot by them was the only one they had known to be killed in the Yehli area. This blockage in communication between big-game hunters and the native inhabitants is a familiar phenomenon in many parts of the world. The natives may be merely apathetic or have their own pertinent reasons, economic or religious, for not wishing to disclose the presence of giant pandas or tigers or jaguars in their 'parish'. As Kermit Roosevelt put it:

Native information required careful checking, for even after a detailed description of an animal, accompanied by a showing of a plate depicting it, we could not rely on a native's word as to its presence in a district. Sometimes this was due to very hazy notions of coloration and the assumption that the white crescent on the black bear's chest entitled it to be called a beishung. At other times misinformation was willful, whether with the common impulse to give pleasant and agreeable news or because the native counted on earning some money as guide before his deception would be discovered.

It is naturally extremely difficult to estimate the distribution and numbers of beishung in their dense bamboo habitat. Even in the 'ideal' tracking-conditions of late autumn one beishung can make so many tracks in the snow and deposit so many droppings, as it wanders around feeding among the bamboo, as to suggest the presence of more beishung than are actually in the vicinity. According to the seasons, so the observer's estimate of the numbers of beishung in a jungle could be totally different. During a month of hunting before the first snows of autumn had fallen on the Chengwai country, for example, Sheldon gained the impression that they were rather rare; but the following month, after snow had fallen, he reversed his opinion and concluded that for such large mammals they were plentiful. From 14 November to 8 December snow covered most of the mountain valleys. During this period Sheldon estimated that within six miles of Chengwai, as the eagle flew, at least six different beishung inhabited scarcely one-tenth of habitable jungle. Elaborating on this estimate he describes how:

Two pandas were seen on 16 November in the Chengwai Valley. I departed two days later for the Mamogon Valley. The latter would not have been reached without crossing the Chengou River valley which was covered with snow, so there is little chance that the two animals referred to could have left the Chengwai Valley and gone to the well-removed Mamogon slopes without our detection. I found unmistakable evidence of three more pandas in the Mamogon valley. The size and location of the tracks offered proof of this statement. Another track was seen far up the valley of the "Da Bei Sgui Gon", and still another just south of the Mamogon and Chengou streams. The day after leaving Mamogon valley, we returned to Chengwai and found the tracks of two giant pandas far up on the east side of the valley. Assuming that these were the same animals as were seen on 16 November, the total would still be six. As a matter of fact I saw fairly fresh panda tracks on almost every slope I hunted after snow had fallen.

Until quite recently it was generally believed that the entire world population of beishung was restricted to an area of only about twenty thousand square miles, extending from the Wassu country around Wenchuan in the north rather more than two hundred miles south to the Yehli district, between the Golden Mountain and the Taliang Shan ranges. Père David's hunters, it will be remembered, captured their beishung in the vicinity of Muping; and this was, and no doubt still is, certainly one of the beishung's strongholds. It was there that Graham obtained his first skin, and there that the Roosevelts found more traces than anywhere else. A second stronghold was in the region of Tatsienlu, where Jack Young obtained his beishung; and a third, the one most frequently visited by Westerners, in the Wassu country around Wenchuan. This was the hunting-ground of Weigold, Schäfer, Sage and Sheldon, Brocklehurst, Graham, Ruth Harkness and Tangier Smith; and it was presumably in this region also that Quentin Young shot his two adults.

All three strongholds lie on the foothills of the Chunglai mountains, which empound the Min and its tributaries. Far to the south of them, almost a hundred miles south-east of Tatsienlu, lie the hamlets of Yehli; but Yehli must not be considered an isolated outpost for, as we have seen, Wilson found traces of beishung in the Wa Shan, fifty miles to the north-east; while Arthur de Carle Sowerby was convinced that they inhabited all the remoter mountainous areas from Yehli southwards into northern Yunnan. Although Sowerby, the founder and curator of the Shanghai Natural History Museum, was a quite remarkably careless reporter he had a very wide knowledge of China and its wildlife, and in this particular estimate he was probably correct, because in 1966 the Chinese announced that a new 'colony' of beishung had been discovered in Yunnan – assuming of course that this report did in fact refer to beishung and not to lesser pandas.

In the north of their range Wilson claimed that beishung were to be found from the great spur of Sungpan, lying to the north of Wenchuan, right through the high mountains to Lungan Fu in the north-east; while Sowerby, again, further extended their range in the east when he 'came across indisputable evidence of the Giant Panda' in the Tapei Shan region of south-west Shensi, two hundred and fifty miles north-east of Chengtu. 'The local takin hunters described its droppings and the places where it had torn up the culms of the bamboos for food.' One wonders why this apparently conclusive evidence of the beishung's presence in this region has been discredited, since no one has disputed the existence of takin in these mountains. It is interesting to note that the remains of a second pre-beishung were unearthed, in 1923, in Pliocene deposits at Wanhsien, not very far south of the Tapei Shan. However, if some of these claims are open to doubt, there is no questioning Pen's Oring Nor record, which makes plausible the 1966 report of beishung in the hills north of Sining; nor Berezovski's Tsingling record, which was circumstantially confirmed by the American botanist Joseph Rock, who informed the Roosevelts that the natives of Tangpu had given him a detailed description of beishung in their country.

We can therefore state with some certainty that the beishung's present range extends for some eight hundred miles from Tsinghai Province (possibly from as far north as Sining) south into northern Yunnan – and in the distant past into upper Burma. If Edgar's and Sowerby's circumstantial evidence of beishung, as far west as Batang and as far east as the Tapei Shan respectively,

A pensive An-An brooding on
events in Moscow. *(Zoological
Society of London)*

123

is accepted, together with the 1966 record of four individuals in an unspecified locality of the Tibetan Himalayas, their east-to-west range may be as much as five hundred miles. The total area of their present habitat may therefore cover some four hundred thousand square miles. True, only a relatively small portion of this range is inhabited, because of their restriction to the limited zones of bamboo jungle; but they are clearly much more widely distributed than has been supposed.

There is every reason to believe that the boundaries of their habitat may be still further extended when China is at peace once more, because Chinese zoologists are well aware of the likelihood of this. Moreover, since their Government introduced complete protection for the beishung in 1949, prohibiting both hunting and the capture of live specimens for export, they have also seen to it that the natives of Szechwan and Sikang understand the reasons for the special interest in their unique 'white bear'. Thus reports from local hunters and officials can be expected to come in more frequently and from hitherto unreported areas. All credit to the People's Republic of China for refusing to profit by exploiting such a potential money-spinner as the giant panda, which even before the last war was valued at $15,000, or thirty lions – Chi-Chi is currently valued at £12,000.

But though the Chinese embargo on the export of beishung may have been imposed only just in time to prevent serious inroads into the stock of a not very numerous animal, with every zoo in the world eager to obtain such a popular exhibit, it is difficult to understand how Chinese sources could have believed until quite recently that the total beishung population did not exceed forty or fifty individuals. Even today Chinese zoologists apparently believe that there are very few of them, though confident that their numbers will increase now that their conservation requirements are better understood. Yet all five beishung in the Peking Zoo in 1956, together with a sixth that died, had been obtained from the same district of Paohsing in western Szechwan. This surely indicated a fair degree of commonness as, at an earlier date, did Tangier Smith's reputed total capture of no fewer than thirteen live beishung. However, they are the men on the spot – give or take a few thousand miles – and they should be in a better position to judge than Western observers, of whom only a handful have ever explored Szechwan and only nine have ever seen a beishung wild in the jungle. But, nevertheless, their estimate would appear to be totally unrealistic, and Desmond Morris's tentative suggestion of several thousand more probable. Actually, if it were possible to obtain an estimate of the total area of bamboo jungle within the beishung's present known range, one should be able to make a rough calculation of their potential population, perhaps basing initial estimates on Schäfer's contention that every beishung occupies a territory of something over a square kilometre in area, or on Sheldon's, that a single animal probably confines its range to one main valley.

One is, of course, curious about the beishung's antecedents. Who were his ancestors? How did he come to be isolated in this relatively small pocket of the earth's most mountainous terrain? Various hypotheses have been advanced to explain these and other problems, but while they are fascinating exercises in detection they are no more than that, though sometimes unwittingly humorous. I shall be merciful and not name the distinguished zoologist, now deceased, who, in discussing the beishung's evolution, affirmed that 'because there were few trees to climb in Hsi-fan, these pandas came down to earth and, no longer needing balancing-poles, discarded the ring tail of the fox for the truncated end which is not the least of the Giant Panda's charms'. Truly, Evolution moves in a mysterious way its wonders to perform!

Almost one hundred years of controversy as to the mammalian family to which the giant panda is most closely related may perhaps be summed up by a story about R. L. Pocock, another eminent zoologist, who was Superintendent of the London Zoo for some years. Before the Roosevelts set out on their expedition to Hsi-fan one of them approached Pocock for any information he could supply concerning the beishung's habits and distribution. Pocock took this opportunity to ask him to obtain certain organs from any beishung he might be fortunate enough to shoot, as he was certain that these particular organs would establish that the beishung was not, as was generally supposed, related either to the bears or to the racoons. The Roosevelts, as we know, did in the event obtain a beishung, which they duly skinned, removing such parts of the carcass as would be required for mounting it in the Chicago Field Museum; but in the excitement of the kill they quite forgot to remove those vital organs requested by Pocock. However, after they had returned triumphantly to camp and were settling down for the night, one of them remembered and, fearing that the carcass would be destroyed by scavengers during the night, conscientiously roused two of the native hunters and returned by lantern-light to recover the missing links. In due course these were handed over to Pocock and 'proved' to the latter's satisfaction that the beishung not only was not related to either the bears or the racoons but did not even belong to the same family as the little panda. In recounting this admirable example of the field collector's integrity Pocock was too gentlemanly to specify the organs that were to afford final proof of the beishung's family relationships – or lack of them; but in this less prudish and most ungentlemanly age it can be revealed that they were the genitals.

However, in the present state of our knowledge no one is in a position to poke fun at Pocock – myself least of any; and on one importantly relevant matter Pocock was quite correct: the genitalia of beishung and bears are so unlike that this dissimilarity virtually rules out the possibility of their being related, despite such strong but superficial physical resemblances as the massiveness of the limbs and the broad, flat feet. In this respect, however, the beishung lacks, as we have seen, the bear's hind heel-pad and, while frequently standing erect, does not walk erect. An additional resemblance is to be found in the fact that the short hair on a beishung's muzzle is directed forward from eyes to nose, as it is in bears and cats but no other carnivores. More significant resemblances between beishung and bears are that the configuration of their brains is identical and that their young are disproportionately minute at birth: only one-nine-hundredth the weight of the female in the case of the beishung, and one-three-hundred-and-fiftieth in, for example, the polar bear. Biologically, however, the only really significant relationship lies in the fact that the beishung's blood-serum is closer to that of the bear than to any other mammal. But, having discovered this significant affinity, and weighed its importance against the dissimilarity of the genitalia, we then learn that the beishung's chromosome-counts not only differ from those of bears but are apparently identical to those of racoons!

To my mind it requires a good deal of imagination to see any physical resemblance between a beishung and a lesser panda, let alone between a beishung and a racoon; or to see the beishung's bold particolouring outlined in the panda's colour-pattern, with red replacing white. Nevertheless, there are unquestionably more fundamental points of resemblance between beishung and lesser pandas than between beishung and bears. Their teeth are very similar. So are their genitalia, though the resemblance in these organs is closer between beishung and racoons than between beishung and pandas. Both beishung and pandas possess ano-genital glandular areas associated with the procedure of scent-marking, which is not a habit of the bears; while the beishung's short intestine and the small size of its liver, gall-bladder and pancreas are also common to the lesser panda. And finally the latter also exhibits some degree of development of the opposable 'thumb', though this could be considered merely the result of a convergence of feeding-habits, since both panda and beishung are bamboo 'pluckers'.

Perhaps, after all, Pocock was right, and the beishung is not closely related to any other mammal.

Scientific Names of Animals Mentioned
in the Text

Bear, Black (Himalayan or Asiatic)	*Selenarctos thibetanus*
Brown	*Ursus arctos*
Polar	*Thalarctos (ursus) maritimus*
Tibetan blue	*Ursus arctos pruinosus*
Deer, Muntjac	*Muntiacus muntjak*
Musk	*Moschus moschiferus*
Père David's	*Elaphurus davidianus*
Tufted	*Elaphodus cephalophus*
White-lipped	*Cervus albirostris*
Dog, Wild	*Cuon alpinus*
Goral	*Naemorhedus griseus*
Leopard	*Panthera pardus*
Lynx, Tibetan	*Lynx lynx isabellina*
Monkey, Golden	*Rhinopithecus roxellanae*
Panda, Giant	*Ailuropoda melanoleuca*
Lesser red	*Ailurus fulgens*
Styan's	*Ailurus fulgens styani*
Pig, Wild	*Sus moupinensis*
Pika (mouse-hare)	*Ochotona thibetana sps*
Racoons	*Procyonidae*
Serow, Chinese	*Capricornis sumatraensis milne-edwardsi*
Sheep, Szechwan blue (bharal)	*Pseudois nahoor szechuanensis*
Takin, Golden	*Budorcas taxicolor bedfordi*
Szechwan	*Budorcas taxicolor thibetana*
Tiger, South China	*Panthera tigris amoyensis*

SELECTED BIBLIOGRAPHY

Note: Much of the literature on the Giant Panda is now repetitive and/or irrelevant or nonsensical. So far as I am aware, every pertinent reference to it or its environment is included here.

BOOKS

The place of publication is London unless otherwise specified.

ALLEN, G. M., *The Mammals of China and Mongolia*, I. New York, 1938.

ANDREWS, R. C., *The New Conquest of Central Asia*, I. New York, 1932.

BURDSALL, R. L., & EMMONS, A.-B. (appendix: J. T. YOUNG), *Men Against the Clouds*. 1935.

CHEN-HUANG, S., *Economic Animals of China*. Peking, 1962.

DAVID, I.'ABBÉ, *La Faune chinoise*. Paris, 1889.

DAVIES, H. R., *Yunnan*. 1909.

FERGUSSON, W. N., *Adventure, Sport and Travel on the Himalayan Steppes*. 1911.

FOX, H. M., *Abbé David's Diary*. Cambridge, Mass., 1949.

HARKNESS, R., *The Lady and the Panda*. 1938.

—— *The Baby Giant Panda*. New York, 1938.

HEUVELMANS, B., *On the Track of Unknown Animals*. 1958.

International Zoo Yearbook, 1966.

JACK, R. L., *Back Blocks of China*. 1904.

JOHNSTON, R. F., *From Peking to Mandalay*. 1908.

LEY, W., *Dragons in Amber*. New York, 1951.

MORRIS, R. & D., *Men and Pandas*. 1966.

PRATT, A. E., *To the Snows of Tibet through China*. 1892.

ROOSEVELT, T. and K., *Trailing the Giant Panda*. New York, 1929.

TATE, G. H. H., *Mammals of Eastern Asia*. New York, 1947.

WALLACE, H. F., *Big Game of Central and Western China*. 1913.

WARD, F. K., *The Land of the Blue Poppy*. 1913.

WENDT, H., *Out of Noah's Ark*. 1956.

WILSON, H. E., *A Naturalist in Western China*. 1913.

JOURNALS

AMUNDSEN, E., 'A Journey through South-west Szechwan'. *Geographical Journal* XV-XVI, 1900.

ANON., 'Panda up a Tree'. *Animal Kingdom* XLV, 1942.

ANON., 'Giant Panda Bred in Peking Zoo'. *China Reconstructs* XIII (3), 1964.

BLAIR, W. R., 'Pandora in her New Home'. *Bulletin of the New York Zoological Society* XLI, 1938.

BROCKLEHURST, H. C., 'The Giant Panda'. *Field* CLXXI, 1938.

—— 'The Giant Panda'. *Journal of the Society for the Preservation of Fauna* XXVIII, 1936.

BÜCHNER, E., & BEREZOVSKI, M., 'Die Säugethiere der Ganssu-Expedition (1884–7)'. *Bulletin de l'Académie des sciences de Saint-Pétersbourg* II (34), 1891.

CARTER, T. D., 'The Giant Panda'. *Bulletin of the New York Zoological Society* XL, 1937.

CHJAN, KH-YU & LIN, L., 'Anatomy of the Digestive System of *Ailuropoda melanoleuca*'. *Acta Zool. Sinica*, 1959.

DAVID, L'ABBÉ, 'Voyage en Chine'. *Nouvelles Archives du Musée de l'Histoire Naturelle* V, Paris, 1869.

—— 'Rapport adressé à MM. les Professeurs-Administrateurs du Musée de l'Histoire Naturelle', 15 Dec. 1871. *Nouvelles Archives* VII, Paris, 1872.

—— Journal d'un voyage dans le centre de la Chine et dans le Thibet Oriental'. *Nouvelles Archives* X, Paris 1874.

DAVIS, D. D., 'The Giant Panda: a Morphological Study of Evolutionary Mechanisms'. *Fieldiana:* Zool. Mem. III, Chicago Natural History Museum, 1964.

DEMMER, H., 'The First Giant Panda since the War has Reached the Western World'. *International Zoo News* V, 1958.

EDGAR, J. H., 'Visiting Muping, the Land of the Giant Panda'. *China Journal of Science and Arts* V, 1926.

—— 'The Haunts of the Giant Panda'. *Journal* of the West China Border Research Society III, Chengtu, 1930.

(Editorial), 'Four Pandas Have Been Found in the Tibetan Himalayas'. *Animals* VII (12), 1966.

ENGELMANN, C.-H., 'Über die Grossäuger Szetschuans, Sikongs und Osttibetts'. *Zeitschrift für Säugertierkunde* XIII (Sonderheft), Berlin 1938.

FU-JEN, C., 'There Are Many Rare Animals in Peking Zoo'. *Zoo Life* II, 1956.

GOSS, L. J., 'How Are the Giant Pandas?'. *Bulletin of the New York Zoological Society* XLV, 1942.

GRAHAM, D. C., 'How the Baby Pandas were Captured'. *Bulletin of the New York Zoological Society* XLV, 1942.

GREGORY, W. K., 'On the Phylogenetic Relationships of the Giant Panda to other Arctoid Carnivora'. American Museum Nov. 878, 1936.

HAAS, G., 'Beitrag zum Verhalten des Bambusbären'. *Zoologischer Garten* XXVII, Leipzig 1963.

HILL, C., 'The Story of Lien-Ho'. *Zoo Life* I, 1946.

HODGSON, B. H., 'On the Cat-toed Subplantigrades of the Sub-Himalayas'. *Journal of the Asiatic Society* XVI, Bengal, 1847.

International Union for the Conservation of National and Natural Resources, 'Giant Panda'. Survival Service Commission Red Data Book, 1966.

JACOBI, A., 'Zoologische Ergebnisse der Walter Stötznerschen Expedition nach Scetschwan'. *Abhandlungen des Berliner Museums* XVI (1 & 2), Dresden, 1923.

JARVIS, C., 'Zoos in China'. *Animals* VIII (17 & 19), 1966.

KAN, O., & SHU-HUA, T., 'In the Peking Zoo – the first baby Giant Panda'.

130

Bulletin of the New York Zoological Society LXVII, 1964.

LEONE, C. A., & WIENS, A. L., 'Comparative Serology of Carnivores', *J. Mammal* XXXVII, 1956.

LOSEBY, R., 'Five Giant Pandas', *Field* CLXXII, 1938.

MATTHEW, W. D., & GRANGER, W., 'New Fossil Mammals from the Pliocene of Szechwan, China'. *Bulletin of the American Museum of Natural History* XLVIII (17), 1923.

MCCLURE, F. A., 'Bamboo as a Panda Food', *J. Mammal* XXIV, 1943.

METTLER, F. A., & GOSS, L. J., 'The Brain of the Giant Panda'. *Journal of Comparative Neurology*, Philadelphia, LXXXIX (1), 1946.

MILNE-EDWARDS, A., 'Extrait d'une lettre de même (M. l'Abbé David) dâtée de la principalité thibetaine (indépendante) de Moupin, le 21 mars 1869'. *Nouvelles Archives* V, Paris, 1869.

MONTAGU, I., 'More about Peking's Panda'. *Animals* III (17), 1964.

—— Letter. *Animals* IV (7), 1964.

MORRISON-SCOTT, T. S. C., 'The Giant Panda'. *Field*, CLXXIII, 1939.

PEN, H-S., 'Some Notes on the Giant Panda'. *Bulletin of the Fan. Memorial Institute of Biology*, Peiping, I, 1943.

——'Animals of Western Szechwan'. *Nature*, CLXXXVI, 1962.

POCOCK, R. I., 'Some external Characters of the Giant Panda'. *Proceedings of the Zoological Society of London*, 1928-9.

——'The Prehensile Paw of the Giant Panda'. *Nature* CXLIII, 1939.

——'The Panda and the Giant Panda'. *Zoo Life* I, 1946.

RAVEN, H. C., 'Notes on the Anatomy and Viscera of the Giant Panda'. American Museum Nov. 877, 1937.

ROOSEVELT, K., 'The Search for the Giant Panda'. *Journal of the American Museum of Natural History* XXX, 1930.

SAGE, D., 'Hunting the Giant Panda'. *China Journal* XXII (1), 1935.

——'In Quest of the Giant Panda'. *Journal of the American Museum of Natural History* XXXV, 1935.

——'In the Land of the Giant Panda'. *Field* CLXVI, 1935.

SCHAEFER, E., 'Der Bambusbär'. *Zoologischer Garten*, Leipzig, X, 1938.

SCHNEIDER, K. M., 'Vom Bambusbären', *Natur und Volk*, Mainz, LXXXII, 1952.

SHELDON, W. G., 'Notes on the Giant Panda'. *J. Mammal* XVIII, 1937.

SICHER, H., 'Masticatory Apparatus in the Giant Panda and the Bears'. Field Museum Publications, Chicago (Zoological Series) XXIX (4), 1944.

SOWERBY, A. DE C., & EDGAR, J. H., 'Giant Panda and Wild Dogs on the Tibetan Border'. *China Journal* II, 1924.

——'The Roosevelts' Expedition in West China'. *China Journal* II (5), 1929.

——'The Pandas or Cat-bears'. *China Journal* XVII (6), 1932.

——'The Pandas or Cat-bears and the True Bears'. *China Journal* XIX (5), 1933.

——'Hunting the Giant Panda'. *China Journal* XXI (1), 1934.

——'Big-game Animals of the Chinese-Tibetan Borderland'. *China Journal* XXV (4), 1936.

131

—— 'A Baby Panda comes to Town'. *China Journal* XXV (6), 1936.

—— 'The Giant Panda's Diet'. *China Journal* XXVI, 1937.

—— 'Another Live Giant Panda'. *China Journal* XXVII, 1937.

—— 'The Lure of the Giant Panda'. *China Journal* XXVIII (5), 1938.

SWINTON, W. E., 'The Giant Panda'. *Illustrated London News* CCVIII, 1946.

TEE-VAN, J., 'Two Pandas – China's Gift to America'. *Bulletin of the New York Zoological Society* XLV, 1942.

WOOD-JONES, F., 'The "thumb" of the Giant Panda'. *Nature* CXLIII, 1939.

—— 'The Forearm and Manus of the Giant Panda'. *Proceedings of the Zoological Society of London* CIX, 1939.

WOODWARD, A. S., 'On the Skull of an Extinct Mammal Related to Aeluropus from a Cave in the Ruby Mines at Mogok, Burma'. *Proceedings of the Zoological Society of London*, 1915.

INDEX

References in *italics* are to
photographs

American Museum of Natural
   History: 26
Amne Machen Shan: 68
Amundsen, Edward: 7
AN-AN: birth, 6; transfer to
   Moscow Zoo, 43, *44*; diet, 80;
   sexual heat, 90, *91*; relations
   with Chi-Chi, 95-7, *98-9*, 100-
   4, 106, *113*, *123*
Andrews, R. C.: *quoted*, 59-60

Bamboo: 5, 23, 47-8, 71; *see also*
   Beishung, food and eating-
   habits
Bayan Kara Shan: 68
Bears: 4, 21-2, 69, 70-1, 125,
   126-7; Asiatic Black, 22, 56-7;
   Brown, 21-2; Koala, 80; Polar,
   118, 126; Tibetan Blue, 22,
   56-7, 68-9
Beishung (Giant Panda): anatomy,
   11, 49, 62-3, 71, 74-5, 105,
   124-7; ancestry, 48, 80-1, 121,
   125-7; ancient records of, 13-
   15; captive individuals, *see under*
   NAMES; catching of, for zoos,
   19, 34-46, 62, 118; climbing
   skill, *50*, 51-2; colouring and
   fur, *12*, 26, 31, 62-3, 85, 106,
   114; disposition, 52, 89-90,
   93-4; 'divinity' of, 48-9; early
   Western knowledge of, 11-33;
   enemies, 56-7, 60, 62; fear of
   dogs, 54-5; food and eating
   habits, 6, 53, 68-9, 71, *72-3*, 74,
   75, 77-9, 83, 86-8, 93; gait, 30,
   31, *32*, 62, 87; habitat and
   range (*see also* Hsi-fan), 4, 6,
   47-8, 49, 67, 69, 120-4;
   hibernation, 106; hunting of,
   15, 18-19, 20-33, 48, 54, 118-

19, 120, 124; intelligence, 53;
   lifespan, 6, 94; liking for honey,
   23, 49; mating, 90-3, 95-104;
   names, 8, 13-14, 48; neighbours,
   63-6; numbers, 117-20;
   protected by law, 124;
   resemblance to other mammals,
   21-2, 31, 53, 62, 63, 82; size
   and weight, *25*, 31, 35, 39, 41,
   103-4, 113-14; sleeping-
   habits, 24, 86, 105; strength and
   suppleness, 54-5, 60, 116;
   value, 124; voice, 24, 92, 97;
   young, 36, *44*, 45-6, 52, 68,
   105-6, *107-11*, 110, 114-16; in
   zoos, 36-7, 38, 86, 95-104
Berezovski, M. M.: 20-1, 67, 69
Boxer Rising: 16
Brocklehurst, Capt. C.: 33, 69,
   92, 104, 106
Bronx Zoo, New York: 34, 39, 40,
   41, 114
Brookfield Zoo, Chicago: 37, 38,
   40, 53

Chengou: 49, 119
Chengou River: 22
Chengtu: 9, 13, 14, 26, 38, 41
Chengwai: 26-8, 87, 90, 119, 120
Chen Liang Shan: 27, 60
Chiang Kai-shek, Mme: 40, 41
Chicago Field Museum: 22, 27,
   126
CHI-CHI: birth, 6; *12*, *32*; tours
   Europe, 43; at London, 49-*51*;
   at Frankfurt, *42*, 53, 54, 77, 80,
   115, 116; eating-habits, 71,
   72-3, 74, *75*, 77, *79*, 80, 86; and
   water, 83, 84, *84-5*; sexual heat,
   90-4, *passim;* relations with
   An-An, 95-7, *98-9*, 100-1, *102*,
   103-4; sleeping habits, 86, 106;
   value, 124
Chiench'ang Valley: 60

133

134